CW00531351

TEACHING THE NATIONAL CURRICULUM (AND MORE) THROUGH DRAMA

TEACHING THE NATIONAL CURRICULUM (AND MORE) THROUGH DRAMA

Sheila Sharpless

Book Guild Publishing
Sussex, England

First published in Great Britain in 2009 by
The Book Guild
Pavilion View
19 New Road
Brighton, BN1 1UF

Typesetting in Times by
Keyboard Services, Luton, Bedfordshire

Printed in Great Britain by
CPI Antony Rowe

A catalogue record for this book is available from
The British Library

ISBN 978 1 84624 341 7

CONTENTS

FOREWORD

Although the title of the book suggests the contents are solely concerned with the National Curriculum, they have, in fact, a far wider purpose. Of course the most important function of the book is to introduce children to the social history of the periods required by the syllabus, and to present it in an interesting and dramatic way. Added to that, however, is the very real benefit of helping them to develop their language skills in reading and writing letters, reports, diaries, articles, essays and poetry. Also, children are encouraged to use a wide variety of speaking techniques, for example explaining, discussing, speech-making, comparing, reporting. As an added bonus for both teacher and pupil, much of the work invites cross curricular teaching, incorporating geography and map reading/making, arithmetic, craft and IT, religious studies, music and choreography.

The children will begin to develop self-confidence when taking on a role, and when they are asking (set) questions of the teacher with regard to the plays. At the same time they are learning, in a different and enjoyable way, something of the past which, whether the National Curriculum continues in its present form or is altered in some way, is still the groundwork for deeper study later on in their school lives.

TEACHING THE NATIONAL CURRICULUM (AND MUCH MORE) THROUGH DRAMA

What is meant by teaching through drama?

Although drama is in a sense a 'subject' to be taught, in educational terms, I prefer to think of it as an enabler, a means of imparting knowledge of many areas. It is essentially an activity, a doing thing, which encompasses not only the mind, but the physical senses, the body, the feelings, the imagination. Through this action, we are able to 'see' and even 'feel' the development of a character or situation and make decisions on the outcome because we have become involved through giving a dramatic 'life' to the study.

For this reason, I have taken the following National Curriculum topics, studied at Key Stage 2:

The Vikings
The Victorians
The Ancient Greeks
The Romans
The Tudors
The Ancient Egyptians
World War 2

and written the information into simple plays, in scenes for ease of lesson planning.

Added to these curriculum topics, I have taken Biblical episodes and historical legends and, again, created dramatic dialogue and modernised the story.

1

The basic texts for these are:

The Good Samaritan (play entitled Third Time Lucky)
The Prodigal Son (play entitled Another Life or The One Who Went Away)
Joseph and the Coat of Many Colours
The Christmas Story

Other topics:

Alfred (the legend) Burning the Cakes
Canute (the legend) Taming the Ocean

Each of the plays is followed by questions and suggested tasks, to test learning.

Finally, I include two games that are to be used to explore contemporary issues.

Who will use this book?

This book is intended to become a shared experience between teacher and pupil; each will find a new way of teaching and learning which should be both educational and enjoyable, and which can encourage a greater understanding of working and learning together. For the children the approach to learning becomes an exciting adventure and for the teacher altogether a better opportunity to know the children in the class in a closer, more social environment, working together to reach an understanding of the topic.

Why do we need this book?

We need the book because it promotes in learning, something which all children do quite naturally from an early age, that is, DOING, ACTING. From the time an infant throws a favourite toy from his pram and expects it to be given back, he is enacting a scene in which, quite unconsciously, he is the 'boss' and the 'giver back' is the underling. The child who has an imaginary friend is 'enacting' a very real relationship. Playing schools, mums and dads, setting up a doll's house or farm yard, imagining monsters, acting out a favourite DVD, playing hide and seek; all these are 'doing things' learning, acting = drama.

I believe passionately that learning through drama has a unique place in the understanding and use of language. By taking part in a play, or exploring a situation through role play, children are taking on the persona of another and in so doing they are experimenting with different patterns of language, and are therefore more able to communicate on many different levels. For example, a young child will use a certain voice when talking to a toy and a different one to parents or friends. In role play, older children are capable of using an extraordinary range of voices to describe, explain or 'become' another person. So, apart from using drama for the enjoyment of learning, it is creating opportunities for language development and communication skills.

How do we begin? How do we go about it?

Clearly we cannot expect children to leap straight into plays, so there must be an introductory period to allow them to be eased into a controlled situation, where they will be taking part in dialogue and acting out characters. In doing so they will be able to learn and remember in more depth.

First we have to accept that drama is 'doing', not talking. It has to be, as far as possible, spontaneous and yet, at the same time, structured. How can this be managed?

There are a number of ways in which the drama sessions

can begin. If it is a new class, the first important act will be to encourage the children in good relationships with each other. Exchanging names (if they are not already known) is more fun if the teacher gives out names such as 'bangers' and 'mash' or 'burger' and 'chips', and the children have to find their 'partner' (they'll soon find real names for themselves). Forming a circle and throwing a bean bag (or similar object) to each other and calling names as they do so is an old trick, but it often works. If, after that, the children seem to be happy with each other, the next stage of introducing drama can begin. For example, the teacher could provide a number of items, such as a hat, a pair of sun glasses, a walking stick, a shawl, a Spanish lace head dress, a necklace. The children would be given or invited to take one and use it to create a character. After a short time, when they have found out what they will be, they can talk about it, or perhaps, if they show sufficient confidence, create a situation in pairs or small groups.

Another idea is telling the children to shut their eyes, then the teacher pretends to throw something on to the floor. The children have to imagine what it could be, find it and do something with it. It could be a toy, a monster, a kitten, a jack in the box, or almost anything. If there are some who find this too difficult, the more adventurous ones could involve him/her in their situation.

Statues. A favourite drama exercise. This is often more fun if done to music. The lesson begins with the children listening to and then moving to music, trying to portray a character. When the music stops, they take up a pose and hold it absolutely still until the teacher has guessed that character.

Other ideas for dramatic activity will come when the plays are about to be used. These will be concerned with the characters and the situations within the play, to ready the children for what follows. Some of the above can be used or adapted for the children in Key Stage 1.

When?

Learning through drama can take place at any time. Ideally a special time-slot allocated to drama is best, but this will depend on the school and the general flexibility of the timetable. If drama is not timetabled, it might have to take place after school. But when the plays are being used as in this book, as part of the curriculum, then of course they will take place within the lesson.

It is at this point, before I demonstrate the method through one of the National Curriculum plays, that I would like to write about some of the books already published on drama in schools. Each of these is written by experienced teachers and each demonstrates the intention to improve the learning experience. All, in my opinion, are interesting and valuable to teacher and pupil.

Drama as a Learning Medium by Dorothy Heathcote (Heinemann)

In the foreword, Cecily O'Neill calls this a ground-breaking book, and I believe it shows an early and basic understanding of the concept of drama in learning. In her chapter 'Code Cracking Literature and Language', Heathcote comes close to my belief in drama as a learning medium, in that she is using it as a tool for understanding literature.

Improve Your Primary School Through Drama by Rachel Dickinson, Jonothan Neelands, and Shenton Primary school (David Fulton)

An exciting book which definitely involves all teachers in the use and teaching of drama. As its title suggests, it covers the whole of the primary school and gives ideas and examples to encourage the use of drama from the nursery child to year 6.

Using Drama to Support Literacy by John Goodwin (Paul Chapman Education Publishing)

Much of the book, as the title suggests, is directed at the children's ability to speak, write and discuss, with thoughtful attention to the development of ability in the use of drama, both in the child and in the teacher, particularly those teachers who are coming to drama in teaching for the first time.

These three above I have studied and of course I am aware there are others. I do applaud their content but I believe that this book introduces the children directly to the use of dramatic dialogue and helps them to remember set texts in a most interesting way, that is by involving themselves in real places and people by doing, rather than simply hearing. I have shown a way of understanding scripture by presenting the characters as real people, not stuffy Bible people of many years before and therefore outdated and boring. This, I hope, gives the teachers a different method of reaching their objectives through the dramatic strategy.

Although the plays are complete in themselves, they do not have to be tackled all at once. The different scenes can be used in accordance with the teacher's understanding of the pupils and their ability. I would like to believe that flexibility is built in to the script, and will make it more satisfying to the teacher as it becomes tailored to her/his children's particular needs.

The development of the play and the questions and tasks which follow are in no way meant to be sacrosanct. They are merely one way of teaching the content, and I expect teachers will find their own ways.

It will be noted that in all of the plays I have referred to the teacher as 'Miss'. I apologise to the male teachers and trust that wherever 'Miss' appears it can be altered to 'Sir'.

6

In all of the plays, the Teacher may be played by the class teacher, an assistant or an older child with above average reading ability.

To add to the educational benefit of the plays, there is much that can be developed in the Design & Technology lessons, such as the making of props and the recognition of skills which will have to be learned.

THE VIKINGS

A play with 34 speaking parts and opportunities for non-readers

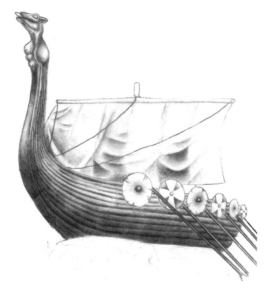

With a picture or drawing of a Viking boat in full view, half the class is invited to sit on one of the mats spread on the floor, sitting close together with their backs to the front of the child behind. These are the Vikings. Grasping imaginary oars, they mime rowing a Viking boat.

The other half of the class is walking up and down at the back of the room. These are the monks. If they could have some kind of cloak, that would make walking different, and if they clasped their hands in prayer, the scene would be set.

After a few minutes, the Vikings leave their boats and crowd together to decide what to do. The monks, after a few more minutes, see the Vikings and begin to run, chased by the Vikings. This is then brought to an end by the teacher and the children are asked to sit down and begin to talk about how they felt in their roles and how they 'saw' each other. The initial questions before each scene are asked quite naturally by the children chosen. Then, when the teacher says, 'Let's meet the family', the room should be arranged as the dwelling of the Scandinavian family. The children are then cast in the roles and the reading begins. At the point, 'They won't know what's hit them,' the Vikings move away.

PROPS needed for this play, made either by the children in design and technology or the IT department: helmets, cloaks, weapons (according to the teacher's discretion), diagram of a Viking boat, logs, pipe cleaners, green sticky tape (for marsh grass), a wine goblet.

Ideally this play needs space, such as the school hall, but if that is not possible, the classroom should be arranged with the chairs in a circle. When the children have sat down, the teacher tells them that for the next few weeks they will be learning about the Vikings.

Obviously each teacher will decide, but I think it could be possible to give out all the roles before the lesson begins, including the children who are going to ask the questions.

Starting the play

CHILD   What is a Viking, Miss?
TEACHER   Vikings were farmers and fishermen and also
             great traders, getting riches from the north,
             such as timber for ship building, iron for

	making tools and weapons, furs for clothing, skins from whales and seals for ship rope and ivory from walruses for carving. Vikings originally came from Scandinavia.
CHILD	Where's that, Miss?
TEACHER	Scandinavia is land which covers Norway, Sweden and Denmark. Later we will find them on the atlas.
CHILD	What was the land like?
TEACHER	It was very harsh land and difficult to farm. But fishing was different. They had plenty of fish, not only for food, but they got oil from them, which they needed for lamps and for oiling their clothing to make it waterproof.
CHILD	Viking is a funny name. What does it mean?
TEACHER	It is believed that it came from *vic*, meaning a sea inlet, for they were surrounded by water, the sea and the fjords.
CHILD	What were their houses like?
TEACHER	Well, let's see if you can imagine one. Let's sit in a circle (*children and teacher do so*). Now, let us imagine we are in a Viking family room. Just one room with a fire in the centre, and a hole in the roof for the smoke to go through. The holes were not always effective and the room became very smoky. In very bad winters, their animals would be brought into the room as well. There were no chairs but perhaps a bench on one side. Now, let's meet the family. The year is about 790 BC.

11

Scene 1

CAST

SOLVIG, the father
SONJE, the mother
FREYA, the daughter
ERIK, the son

SOLVIG	Erik, put some more wood on the fire. We'll all feel warmer with a good fire burning. It's just as well we collected all that wood from the forest to see us through the coldest days.
SONJE	Yes, and Freya, while Erik is doing that, you can make some light straws for us. The reeds are over there in the corner. Erik can help you when he's finished putting wood on the fire, and between you, you'll soon be done. We need plenty of wicks for the lamps. Solvig, have we plenty of fish oil?
SOLVIG	We have. We have had good catches lately, as you know.
	(*Freya goes to the corner of the room and brings some reeds or marshstraw as they called it. She begins to mime peeling away the outer covering.*)
FREYA	Come on, Erik. You were told to help me.
ERIK	Why do I always have to help her? Why can't she do anything by herself?
SONJE	Because you are older, so stop grumbling. And get on with it.
ERIK	Oh all right, but next time you can help me with the logs. (*He ducks as his father takes a swipe at him.*)

12

SOLVIG   That's enough, Erik. Now sit down and behave.
            (*Erik sits on the floor and sulks.*)

TEACHER   So, you see they each had tasks to do and
            they could be just as difficult as you can be.
CHILDREN   Oh, Miss, we're not difficult.
TEACHER   Aren't you?
CHILDREN   NO!
TEACHER   All right. But now, let us continue.
CHILD   What did they do? Apart from farming and
            fishing?
TEACHER   Well, we know about them from the thirteenth
            century BC, when they began to want to travel,
            to trade with other people. They built wonderful
            boats, some of which held twenty men, good
            strong rowers who could make them travel very
            fast.
CHILD   What were the boats like, Miss?
TEACHER   Long and slender. High in the front, called the
            prow, and at the back, called the stern. Have a
            look at the picture. But, gradually, the Vikings
            became restless and wanted not just trade but
            riches and so their journeys became raids, which
            began in AD 793, when they attacked a monastery
            at Lindisfarne, an island just off Scotland's coast.
            Listen now and you will hear them planning.

Scene 2

CAST

THOR
ODIN
OLAF
OTHER (NON-SPEAKING) CHILDREN WHO ARE CAST AS THE
VIKINGS.

13

ODIN	It's time we did more than trading. We've travelled far; spent our time constructing more and better boats, so now we can go further and begin to gain riches.
OLAF	You're right. Trading is all right but it doesn't make us rich.
THOR	Money, gold and silver. I can just see it. Lots of it. We could be the richest people in the world.
ODIN	Well, that's true, but we must plan. I know you, Thor, you're so hot-headed you'd plunge in before thinking about it.
THOR	It's better than being too slow like you, Odin. If we left it to you we'd never get anywhere.
OLAF	That will do, you two. Fast or slow we must plan, so stop your quarrelling and let us think.
ODIN	Right, now where is the kind of place we could begin our raids?
THOR	I've heard that places where Christian priests live have great riches.
ODIN	Yes that's right. When they join the monastery I've heard they give it all their money.
THOR	What nonsense. Who would give everything away? Talk sense.
ODIN	I am talking sense and if you don't apologise I'll, I'll – (*He puts up his fist to Thor.*)
OLAF	Will you two stop arguing? I'm sick of you. We'd be better to stay at home.
THOR	No, no, we must plan.
ODIN	All right. Lets all think. (*Silence*)
ODIN	(*after a moment*) You say a monastery would be a good place to start. But where is the nearest one?
OLAF	A place called Lindisfarne off the coast of Scotland.

THOR	And this is wealthy?
OLAF	Yes, very.
ODIN	Then let us prepare. Come, let us begin. We'll catch them unawares. They won't know what's hit them!

(They go off, laughing evilly.)

Questions

1. Find on your atlas the places mentioned in scene 1. If the children are able, they could fill in Lindisfarne on an outline map of the UK.
2. Where were the Vikings planning to raid first?
3. Who seemed to be the boss of these Vikings?

Before the next reading begins, the room should, as far as possible, be arranged to represent the monks' garden,

TEACHER	So now, let's see the monks at Lindisfarne. They are walking in their garden.

Scene 3 The Monastery

CAST

BROTHER JOHN
BROTHER JAMES
BROTHER PETER
ODIN
OLAF
THOR
MONKS
VIKINGS } NON-SPEAKING CHILDREN

JAMES	It's a beautiful morning, Brother John. How

15

	lovely the garden is. The herbs which Brother Matthew tends are looking very good.
JOHN	Yes, Father Abbott was saying only yesterday that he has heard of some new herbs which Brother Matthew would like to plant.
JAMES	I'm sure they will do well, Brother Matthew is a good gardener. We are very lucky to have him.
JOHN	We are, for I am sure that our meals would be less tasty without his herbs to flavour them.
JAMES	That is true. We are so fortunate. God has been very good to us.
JOHN	Indeed, indeed. And we have the added blessing of St Cuthbert's mortal remains here with us at Lindisfarne.
	(*There are sounds of commotion, shouting and running feet. Suddenly Brother Peter rushes in.*)
PETER	(*out of breath*) Brother John, Brother James. Oh, may the Lord bless us. Oh. Oh!
JOHN	Good gracious, Brother Peter. Whatever is the matter? You are so out of breath and as white as a sheet. What is it?
PETER	Oh, dreadful news. Terrible. There are boats, hundreds of them. Coming towards us. Oh and, and –
JAMES	Pull yourself together, Brother Peter. If you have anything to tell us do so now please.
PETER	Yes, well, Brother Philip and I were seeing to the bees in the garden, when I looked out to sea and, oh dear, what did I see?
JOHN	Well? What? What did you see?
PETER	Boats, lots of boats. High in the front with monsters on the top. And men, many men. Terrifying. They are coming to attack us! Oh dear!
JAMES	This sounds serious. Come, Brother John, let

16

JOHN
us look. (*They run to one side.*) Oh look. I think he's right. They're going to attack us. Hurry, there's no time to be lost. Brother Peter, run to the Father Abbott. Tell him we are about to be attacked. Then call the brothers. They must clear the altar and go to the library and hide the illustrated texts. Oh, may St Cuthbert and all the saints preserve us.
(*The shouting is now louder.*)

JAMES
Come, we must hide.
(*As they begin to rush off, the Vikings rush in at speed.*)

ODIN
Not so fast. (*He grabs Brother James by the collar.*) Tell us where you keep the valuables.

JAMES
Never.

ODIN
You will, or be prepared to meet your maker.

OLAF
(*He has Brother Peter by the arm.*) Come on, little priest, take me to the gold. (*He drags Brother Peter off.*)

THOR
(*chasing Brother John*) Come back here. (*They run off. Other monks run in, pursued by the Vikings.*) You will come with us. But first, the treasures from your vaults. Or we will torch your monastery like we torched your stupid church. Come on, men. Get them and if they resist they'll come with us as slaves. (*He goes off, dragging Brother John.*)
    (*If there are sufficient children playing monks and Vikings, more running and shouting may continue.*)

OLAF
Bring them back to the boats with the treasures. We've done well. Next raid, Orkney, then Shetland and Iona. Oh, there are many more places we can plunder. More wealth, more slaves. We are magnificent.

VIKINGS   (*Shouting*) We are magnificent! To the boats. (*They run off taking with them Brother James, Brother Peter and any other monks. Shouting for joy. After they have gone, there is silence for a while, then Brother John gets up from the floor, clothes untidy, looking very scared. He looks round, and seeing that he is alone, runs off.*)

TEACHER   Well, poor Brother John, but at least he escaped those Vikings. They really must have been very frightening with their murderous weapons. They were very heavy too, made of iron. The Vikings prized their weapons above all things. The swords, in particular, were very grand, often encrusted, or inlaid with silver. Until they became Christians, they often had their swords buried with them.

CHILD   Before they were Christians, what were they?

TEACHER   Well, they believed that there were three great worlds which were to them sort of gods. There was Earth, called Midgara. Under earth to the north was called Nyetheim, where the monster called Hel lived in deep endless darkness. Above earth was Asgard, the shining home of the gods.

CHILD   Well, who were their gods?

TEACHER   Odin, Thor and Trigg. Odin was top of the chief group, called Midgara, Trigg was the mother of the gods, and Thor was their son. Then gradually they gave up these gods when they became Christian, and by the eleventh century Shetland and the Orkney Islands had also become Christian.

CHILD   Did they always fight?

TEACHER   Yes, for a long time they did, but they were
           badly beaten in battles that took place from
           840 to 860. Yet fifteen years later they were
           building even bigger boats and then they had
           an enormous fleet and hundreds of men and
           they won a lot of our country in battle, including
           East Anglia and London, and the English kings
           were put to death. But nine years later King
           Arthur, who had not been killed, took back
           London. We will find out more about him in
           the next scene.

Questions

1. Write about the family in Scene 1 and describe their house.
2. Imagine you are Brother John and describe in writing
   the fight with the Vikings, and how he managed to get
   away.

As before, the children are seated with the teacher who
reminds them of the previous scene (3) before introducing the
one now to be played and casting the children in the various
roles.

   This time they could be allowed to plan the room as they
think fit for a King.

Scene 4

CAST

KING ARTHUR
SOLDIER SERVANT
GUITHORM

KING ARTHUR has called his army together.

19

ARTHUR   (*talking to his army*) It is essential that we retake London. It cannot remain in the hands of the Viking people. Send for their leader Guthorm and we will have a discussion. Go. (*While he waits, Arthur sits and writes on a scroll. One of the soldiers brings him a goblet of wine.*)

SOLDIER   Wine, Sire?

ARTHUR   Ah, yes, thank you.

GUITHORM   (*entering*) Greetings, noble King. I was but a few yards away. Your summons is urgent?

ARTHUR   It is. I feel that we must cease our constant warfare. Would you agree?

GUITHORM   I do, but I have reservations. I must know your plan before I make any agreement.

ARTHUR   Of course, but first, will you take some wine?

GUITHORM   I will.
                (*Arthur signals to his servant who bows, reaches for the wine bottle, and brings a goblet of wine to Guthorm.*)

GUITHORM   (*takes the goblet and nods*) Now, Arthur, your plan.

ARTHUR   I propose that we divide England into two parts.

GUITHORM   Not too pleased with that idea.

ARTHUR   But wait. A line can be drawn from Shoebury in the South East to Cheddar in the west and into part of Northumbria in the centre covering York. That would be your area, which I shall call Danelaw, and the rest will belong to England. What say you?

GUITHORM   It seems you have it all planned, even to the title of our section. Well, if it will stop the bloodshed, I will agree. Shall we shake hands?

ARTHUR   We will (*they shake hands*). This calls for a celebration. (*He calls to his servant.*) We will walk in the garden. Bring more wine. (*The servant bows and goes off as Arthur and Guthorm go off in another direction.*)

TEACHER   Well, that seemed all right, didn't it? But not for long, for between 900 and 937 the English recaptured Danelaw, thinking that would make peace in the land. But in 939 the Norse Vikings from Dublin invaded and beat England. From then on, England became one country and the Norse Vikings stayed on.

CHILD   But did it stay peaceful then, Miss?

TEACHER   I'm afraid not. In 980 the Vikings attacked again. In the next scene you'll find out what happened.

Questions

1. In pairs, imagine you are Arthur and Gulthorm and discuss the Danelaw.
2. Ask your music teacher to find some music which might illustrate angry Vikings, and, with a group, choreograph a dance.
3. Write a poem about the Vikings.

As usual the children are seated, waiting for the teacher to assign the roles.

At the end the children could try to make the men sound very angry. As they go off they shake their fists in the air as they shout 'Down with the English!'

21

Scene 5

CAST

ABI
AEGIN
BORG ⎫ A group of Norse Vikings
EILAF
GUTHRED
NON-SPEAKING VIKINGS

ABI	I tell you, something must be done. The English have ruled for too long.
AEGIN	You say true, Abi. They must be taught a lesson.
BORG	Our people had to suffer the Danelaw.
EILAF	And then the English took back what they had given.
GUTHRED	Talking is all very well, but what are we to do about it?
ABI	Our bases in Normandy, and our huge army should make it easy to attack England again.
BORG	Yes, they think they have won, but I think that now...
EILAF	...it's our turn. (*Murmurs from all*, 'Yes, yes, so it is.')
GUTHRED	So we are all agreed.
ABI	All that remains then is to decide when.
BORG	And how.
EILAF	The tide will be important, and the weather.
GUTHRED	We need a strong wind to fill our sails.
ABI	And little moonlight.
BORG	Yes, for under cover of darkness we'll make a surprise attack.
EILAF	Then come. Let us put our plan into action.
ALL	(*shouting angrily*) Down with the English!

Questions

1. Later, England took away the Danelaw from the Vikings and then paid them to stay away. If the area was 200 square miles and the English gave £1.50 for each square mile, how much would they have had to pay?
2. Draw a fleet of Viking longboats some with square sails.

The teacher reminds the children of how the previous scene ended, and assigns roles.

TEACHER   And so, once again, England was attacked. There were dreadful battles and many casualties. It was in 980 and after the battles, the English decided to pay the Vikings to stay away. Huge amounts of silver were paid to them but it did not last, for thirty years later the Vikings attacked again, this time under a new leader called Sweyn and his son Cnut. Fighting continued until Edmund, the English King, died and then the Viking Cnut became King of England.

CHILD   What happened next, Miss?

TEACHER   Well, the Vikings became Christians, built churches and mixed well with the English, speaking their language.

CHILD   When the men were fighting, and after, what did their wives do?

TEACHER   That's a good question. The women, as well as keeping house, used to weave material from wool and silk on large upright looms. They also made jewellery. The Vikings all loved fine things. Clothes of fine wool, tablecloths, silver goblets, white bread were all signs of nobility. A noble would wear a fine wool cloak,

	decorated with silk or silver borders over a tunic of wool, fine leather boots and a fur hat. The women wore an underdress of wool and an overdress, rather like a pinafore dress, fastened at the neck with large gold buttons.
CHILD	Where did they get all the material?
TEACHER	They travelled and traded in many countries.

Scene 6

CAST

EGIL
BLANE
GISMUNG
HANSO
FOREIGN SOLDIERS (NON-SPEAKING)

EGIL	I tell you all again, we need timber for our boats.
BLANE	All right Egil, you think of nothing but boats. What about some walrus ivory for our carving?
GISMUNG	What? We've got plenty of that. Are you being soft in the head? What we need are slaves to do our work for us.
BLANE	Who are you calling soft in the head? How dare you? (*He goes to attack Gismung.*)
HANSO	Stop! Save your fighting. We've got to make sure of *all* the things we want – and I think it's going to be difficult.
EGIL	You're right. And here comes trouble, I think we're not wanted here in Constantinople. (*Some foreign soldiers advance on them.*)
HANSO	Fight, men. Don't give in. (*A fight ensues for a minute or two, then the*

foreigners run away, leaving the Vikings looking pleased with themselves.)

EGIL   Well, I'm glad our trading partners aren't all like that.

HANSO   What if they were? Vikings always win.

TEACHER   Well, I'm not sure that's true. But that must be the end, children. Later there will be some work for you to complete, which I'm sure you will do well.

Questions

1. Draw either a noble's outfit or a woman's dress.
2. With a partner, hold a conversation about a) the day's work (women) or b) a set of clothes (men).
3. Imagine you are a Viking and write a letter to a friend, telling him/her about the battle that took place at Lindisfarne.
4. Name three things the Vikings needed from the traders.
5. In what place were they when they fought with the traders?

Research Sources

The Vikings in Britain by Robert Hull (Wayland)
Viking by Susan M. Margeson (Dorling Kindersley)
Blood of the Vikings by Julian Richards (Hodder & Stoughton)
Lindisfarne; The Cradle Island by Magnus Magnusson (The History Press)

THE VICTORIANS

A play in seven scenes

Many speaking parts but opportunities also for poor or non-readers

PROPS needed for this play:

Scene 1 A walking stick for the Queen and a shawl. Prince Albert could also carry a cane or stick and perhaps a copy of *The Times* newspaper.

Scene 2 A large cage-like structure for the mine (I have suggested chairs for this within the script but a 'cage' would make the experience more real), maybe one or two miners' lamps, a cart for the hurryers to pull, a screen depicting the seam of coal, black and dark to be used as a backdrop. Bags of bread and a container for tea for each of the children. Other objects will occur to the teacher in the preparation. These are merely suggestions.

Scene 3 In the drawing room scene, there could be (if furniture is not possible) an atmosphere of over-crowding. A large clock, an aspidistra and other potted plants. A stuffed bird perhaps a table covered in a plush cloth. Whatever is chosen the idea is to represent the typical crowding of objects in a Victorian drawing room. If costumes are available, at about 1850 the ladies would be wearing full-skirted crinolines. The men would probably be wearing tight trousers with a smoking jacket. Again, these are just suggestions to give the pupils a 'feel' for the period.

Starting the play

When the children have come in to the classroom, the teacher tells them that for the next few weeks, they will be learning about the Victorians.

First, the children (already selected) are asking questions and then we have a mini-scene in which Queen Victoria and Prince Albert are talking about where they would like to live.

CHILD 1   Miss, who were the Victorians?
CHILD 2   And why were they called that?

TEACHER	They were called Victorians because they lived at the time of Queen Victoria's reign.
CHILD	She was our Queen's grandmother, wasn't she?
TEACHER	Great, great grandmother.
CHILD 2	Was that hundreds of years ago, Miss?
CHILD 1	Were you living then, Miss?
TEACHER	No I wasn't, thank you very much and no, it wasn't hundreds of years, but it is over one hundred years since Queen Victoria died, and she was Queen for sixty years.
CHILD 2	Was she married, Miss?
TEACHER	Yes, she was married to a German Prince called Albert.
CHILD 1	A German Prince? (*Child begins a goose step. The others laugh.*) Sorry, Miss. Where did she live?
TEACHER	Well, she had several places to live, listen.

Scene 1

CAST

QUEEN VICTORIA
PRINCE ALBERT

BRIGHTON PAVILION

(*Enter Queen Victoria and Prince Albert*)

QUEEN	Oh Albert, I do like living by the sea here in Brighton, but I am beginning to dislike the Pavilion.
PRINCE	But you used to like it. You often said how delightful it is.
QUEEN	I know, but I have found that people keep staring at us through the windows.

29

PRINCE   Well, if you are really worried about it, we could remove to Windsor, or Balmoral, or even Buckingham Palace.

QUEEN   Yes, but not permanently. I would like to think of Balmoral as a place for holidays. Windsor is delightful but only for short visits and Buckingham Palace needs such a lot of building work to make it habitable. No, I like to be near the sea, and it's better for the children.

PRINCE   We shall think of something. I'll talk to the Prime Minister, Mr Robert Peel. I'm sure he will be sympathetic to Your Majesty. You know he would want you to be happy.

QUEEN   Yes, I do know, but Albert, of all the places we have visited, the little Isle of Wight pleased me the most. And I enjoy the journey. Our special royal train to Southampton and then the pretty little paddle steamer to Cowes. So enjoyable. Perhaps Mr Peel could find us a home there.
            (*They go off.*)

CHILD   Did they live on the Isle of Wight, Miss?
TEACHER   Yes, eventually they found a farmhouse near Cowes, with beautiful grounds going down to the sea. They called it Osborne House and Prince Albert made plans to enlarge it. The Queen and her daughters, the Princesses, used to bathe from a bathing machine which is still there today. So is the house and a lovely little building called the Swiss Cottage, especially given by the Swiss people for the royal children.
CHILD   What's a bathing machine, Miss?
TEACHER   Well, it's a bit like a beach hut on wheels which go on runners, rather like a railway line.

30

	The Queen goes inside with her lady-in-waiting and gets dressed in her bathing suit and then the little machine is pulled to the water.
CHILD	Did she wear a bikini, Miss?
TEACHER	No, I'm afraid not. Her bathing suit was like a very large frock and she wore shoes and a hat.
CHILD	A hat? For swimming? Oh Miss. (*This gets the children laughing again.*) Was it like a bath hat?
TEACHER	No, actually it was like a real hat, with a brim. I think she must have found it hard to keep on. (*More laughs as the children imagine swimming with a hat on.*)
CHILD	That was funny and I liked hearing about the Queen, but what about the people? Poor people and people like us?
TEACHER	Ah yes. Unfortunately there were very many poor people at the time. Not like you, but children as young as four years of age had to

	work long hours in the mines and factories. They had dreadful lives.
CHILD	We wouldn't be allowed to work at that age, would we, Miss? What did they do?
TEACHER	Listen to the next part of the play. I think you'll understand then.

Questions

1. In pairs, draw a picture of Osborne House. First, as you think it might have been as a farmhouse, and then as it is now (from the picture), drawn to a scale of 1 in 5 cms.
2. Draw a picture of a lady in a ball gown.
3. Find out what dances and music the Victorians enjoyed and choreograph a dance for your group.
4. By drawing cut-outs of furniture, flowers, rugs etc, design a typical Victorian drawing room.
5. Today, the cost of visiting Osborne House is £5.50 for adults and £2 for children. Teachers pay only £1. If twenty-five children were taken there by five teachers, what would it cost to go in?

Scene 2

CAST

FIVE CHILDREN
THREE ADULTS
FOREMAN

(*The foreman is hustling five children and three adults into a small cage which will take them down to the coal face.*)

CHILD 1	Oh don't, you're hurting me.

CHILD 2	I can't help it. We're always squashed up in here.
ADULT	You kids, shut up whining, we'll be going down in a minute.
CHILD 3	Dad, I'm tired. What's the time?
ADULT 2	The usual time to start, 4 am.
CHILD 3	But I didn't get to bed till eleven.
CHILD 4	Nor did I. Ow, get off my foot.
CHILD 1	Well stop pushing me.
ADULT 3	Now, you got your bread and your jug of tea?
CHILD 5	Yes, and I'm hungry now.
ADULT 3	Well, you'd better not eat it now, you'll need it later.
ADULT 2	Hang on, we're going down.
	(*There is silence for a moment, and then*)
CHILD 5	I hate going down. My stomach feels as if it's falling out.
ADULT 3	Now the day begins. Look out, here's the foreman.
FOREMAN	Right, come on then. You two, children one

	and two, you'll be hurrying. Know what that is, do you?
CHILD 1	Yes, Sir, pulling the coal cart.
FOREMAN	Right then, get that rope round one of you and the other one get to the back of the cart and push. Remember, keep your heads down. The roof's only 18 inches above you.
	(*Children one and two crouch down and begin to pull and push an imaginary cart.*)
CHILD 1	I hate this. You push and I'll pull.
FOREMAN	Shut up and get on with it. Now, child three, you're a carrier. Go on one of you, put the backit on his back while he bends down. Right, off you go. Come on you men, get on with cutting the coal out, then the kid can carry it. Make it a few more hundredweight today. You'll do it if you don't slack as you usually do. Child four, you're a pump boy. Get on with it. (*To Child 5*) You're the littlest and a girl, you can be a trapper.
CHILD 5	I don't want to.
FOREMAN	Shut up. You don't have to do much, just open the air doors and let the carts go through.
CHILD 5	But I'll be all alone in the dark. The water drips on me and sometimes the rats come and eat my bread.
	(*Child 5 goes and mimes opening a heavy door.*)
CHILD 4	I was a pump boy last week. I hated it. The water rose up so high I had to run for my life.
FOREMAN	Quiet you. Any more of your lip and you'll feel my strap. Get on with it.
	(*Child 4 crouches down and begins to mime working a pump, up and down, faster and faster, until he has to run away.*)

FOREMAN   Come back 'ere, you little devil.

CHILD 4   I can't, won't. The water'll drown me.

FOREMAN   Just let me catch you, you...

(Child 4 skips away making faces at the foreman. The rest of the children laugh.)

FOREMAN   I'll give you what for. Come 'ere.

(Child 4 turns to run but falls over. Just as the foreman reaches him one of the adults grabs him and glares at the foreman, who turns away.)

FOREMAN   Good thing it was you who caught 'im. I'd a flayed 'im alive. Now, get on with it all of yer.

ADULT 1   I can't take much more of this. The way the kids are treated. I'll get him one of these days.

ADULT 2   Easy my friend. We don't want trouble.

ADULT 3   He's right though. They shouldn't be treated so badly. It's just as bad in the factories.

ADULT 2   Except it's cleaner in the factories. They don't get coal dust in their little lungs.

ADULT 1   Their hours are far too long – it's bad enough for us, but worse for them.

ADULT 2   I've heard talk of someone in government trying to reduce hours to ten a day.

ADULT 3   That's a dream. I bet it won't happen.

FOREMAN   Talking, are you? Slackers. Want your pay cut? Get on and cut that coal or you'll be sorry.

TEACHER   What a horrid man. But thank you, children, you did that well. In fact, the days *were* reduced to ten hours; even that sounds a lot. But, gradually things got better for the children, and the same man who wanted a ten-hour day, a man called Lord Ashley, the Earl of Shaftesbury, eventually made it possible for education for every child. Sunday school had been available for some time, although most children were too tired to attend, but it was in Queen Victoria's time that all children under the age of ten had to attend school every day.

Questions

1. In a pair, make conversation between
   (a) The foreman and his wife when he gets home, telling her about his day and
   (b) one of the children and his/her mother/father/friend about the day in the mine.
2. Write a poem about the mine.
3. The children in the mine would probably earn one penny a day. A loaf of bread would have cost three pennies. If a family of three children needed six loaves a week how many days would the children have to work to buy these?
4. What do you think a 'backit' is used for?

TEACHER   Now we will find out something about a different kind of society. These people are what was known as 'upper class' and this is just one event in their lives. So let us listen to them.

Scene 3

CAST

SIR GEORGE ASHTON
LADY ASHTON
MR PAXTON
PENELOPE
CECILY

An upper-class drawing room where a party is about begin.

LADY ASHTON   I have invited only a few close friends this evening. A small gathering, I fancy.

PENELOPE   Oh, Mama, small parties are so boring.

CECILY   I agree. I like large parties with lots of nice young men.

LADY ASHTON   Child, that's not the kind of comment a well brought up young lady should make.

PENELOPE   I should like a really grand ball.

CECILY   Oh yes, a ball. Oh, Mama, can we have one?

LADY ASHTON   Indeed. Of course we shall have a ball for your coming out, Penelope.

CECILY   But that's next season. Can't we have a ball sooner? Even a small one?

PENELOPE   There's Papa over there talking so earnestly to Mr Paxton. Will you ask him?

LADY ASHTON   I will when he has finished his conversation. I'll just move across to him.

37

SIR GEORGE	And this young fellow Brunel. Making a name for himself, I understand.
MR PAXTON	He certainly is. Not only has he designed an iron bridge –
SIR GEORGE	An iron bridge?
MR PAXTON	Yes, and now an iron ship.
SIR GEORGE	My word, an iron ship. And does he expect it to float?
MR PAXTON	He does. At present she is in Bristol docks and Mr Brunel is convinced she will cross the Atlantic under steam.
SIR GEORGE	And what does he call this iron ship?
MR PAXTON	She is to be called the SS *Great Britain.*
SIR GEORGE	Hmm. Well, bless my soul. Lady Ashton, my dear, what amazing news Mr Paxton has just given me. Er, you wanted to talk to me?
TEACHER	And there we must leave them.

Questions

1. Draw a picture of the SS *Great Britain*.
2. Write your idea of the conversation between Sir George and Lady Ashton about the ball Penelope and Cecily want.
3. If Penelope and Cecily get their way and a ball is arranged, calculate the cost of the following:
   Hotel ballroom   £100
   Food and drink for 75 guests @ £10 each
   Dress for Lady Ashton   £25
   Dress for Penelope   £19
   Dress for Cecily   £19
   How much would that come to?
   How much change would there be from £1,000?

TEACHER	You have acted in scenes with different people: royalty, the poor and the rich. Now, we are going to find out about another section of society. The unwanted and unloved; the homeless and the poorest in the land.
CHILD	Who were they, Miss?
CHILD	Why were they unloved?
CHILD	Where did they go?
TEACHER	They were taken to a place called a workhouse.
CHILD	You mean like our school? That's a workhouse. (*Laughter*)
TEACHER	I see your point, but no, not like your school. Much much worse (*groans from the children*).
CHILD	Tell us, Miss. Why were people there?
CHILD	And what was the place like?
TEACHER	The building was usually of dark-red brick with small windows. And they were there either because they had no parents or home, or because their parents could not look after them. But listen and you will understand.

Scene 4: The workhouse

CAST

MR BEEDLE, warden of the workhouse
MRS BEEDLE, his wife
MARY ANN, homeless child
FREDDY, her brother
ALICE, also an inmate

MR BEEDLE	You can see the miserable specimens that come to us.
MRS BEEDLE	Indeed I do. (*To Mary Ann and Freddy*) Stand up straight when you are in front of your betters. And don't sniff.
FREDDY	Sorry, ma'am. I can't help it.
MR BEEDLE	You can and you will, you wretched child. And you (*to Mary Ann*), what are you crying for?
MARY ANN	I d-don't like it here.
MRS BEEDLE	Oh don't you? You should be grateful that we have given you a home, with food and shelter. You ungrateful little brat.
MR BEEDLE	Yes. I think she'd better learn how to be grateful. No supper for ungrateful children.
FREDDY	That's cruel. I think you're horrid. She's hungry. We haven't had anything to eat since yesterday and you're, you're beastly.
MRS BEEDLE	Well I never! Such rudeness, such ungodly behaviour. You can go supperless to bed also. Off you go. (*The children run off straight into the arms of Alice. Mr and Mrs Beedle go off the other way.*)
ALICE	Well, well. You've upset the Beedles.

40

MARY ANN   (*sobbing*) Y-y-yes.
FREDDY   I hate them, they're horrible.
ALICE   Shh. Don't let them hear you. Come on,
            I'll take you to the dormitory. Then I'll
            get some food to you, somehow.

TEACHER   Well, the poor children. I hope they got some
            food after all. Alice saved them, didn't she?
            There is one very famous workhouse child in
            one of Mr Charles Dickens' books. His name
            was Oliver Twist. He was always hungry, but
            when he asked for more porridge at breakfast
            time, he got into awful trouble.
CHILD   It must have been a terrible experience, Miss.
            Are there still workhouses?
TEACHER   No. They were closed a long time ago and
            many of them were turned into hospitals but
            eventually they were pulled down, after the
            Second World War. But strangely, quite recently
            a report has been published which tells of
            experiences in a workhouse, written by children.
            Many of them say life in a workhouse could
            have been worse, since they worked in factories
            all day and returned at night. Most agreed that
            it was better than the dreadful conditions at
            home. But there we must leave them. We have
            three more scenes, which will be about Victorian
            family life.

Questions

1. Write a poem about the workhouse.
2. What is a dormitory?
3. Who was the kindest person in the workhouse scene?
4. Why were the children hungry?

TEACHER   As we have seen when we compared the life of Penelope and Cecily with the children in the mine, class in the Victorian times was important. Everyone knew their class and, as they said, 'their place in life'. If you were poor and working class you were expected to respect those who were rich and were upper class, or middle class. As you read in 'The Workhouse', Mrs Beedle told the children to 'stand up in front of your betters'. If you were upper class you would have several servants, middle class probably one or two, working class, none; the mother would look after the family, balance the small amount of money her husband brought in, do the housework, mending, cooking, in fact everything. Let us first look at a well-off family and see the children with their nurse, often referred to as Nanny.

Scene 5

CAST

NANNY
VICTORIA
STANLEY
ETHEL
ALFRED

VICTORIA   Nanny, Stanley has had two turns on the rocking horse and I haven't had one yet today.

NANNY   Now Master Stanley, let your sister have a turn.

STANLEY   Oh all right, but she did have it nearly all the morning yesterday.

NANNY   Well, now it's today, so you must share.

ETHEL	Nanny, can you please help me dress my doll? I can't do it.
NANNY	Yes, but what am I always telling you? There's no such word as can't. You can if you try.
ALFRED	When is Cook going to send up our dinner? I'm hungry.
NANNY	Soon. I expect James the footman or Emmy the parlour maid will bring it.
STANLEY	And after dinner, can we walk to the park? I want to sail my little boat.
ETHEL	And I want to take my dolly out in her dolly's pram.
VICTORIA	Can I take my skipping rope?
ALFRED	I shall take my hoop.
TEACHER	These upper-class children lived a comfortable life, waited on by a Nanny and their dinner brought to them. And all their toys. They were luckier than the middle class. A shopkeeper expected his children to work in the shop as soon as they were old enough. Let's take a look at a grocer's shop, with one of the older children helping.

Questions

1. How many toys did the children have?
2. What was it that Nanny was always telling Ethel? Why?
3. Who were James and Emmy?
4. Write a short story about what the children were going to do in the park.

Scene 6

CAST

MR ROBINSON
DICK, his son
JOAN, his daughter

MR ROBINSON	Now, Dick, get down that large tin of tea leaves. Mrs Smith will be in in a minute and she always buys a quarter of a pound of tea on Wednesdays.
DICK	Right, Dad. Coo, it's ever so heavy.
MR ROBINSON	Be careful now. Don't drop it. Joan, stop day-dreaming and get some blue sugar bags and weigh out a few half pounds. Can you do that?
JOAN	Course I can.
MR ROBINSON	Well don't be long. It's nearly dinner time and we have to close the shop.

DICK	I know, and I'm hungry.
JOAN	So am I.
MR ROBINSON	Your sister Ruth will be down soon to tell us that your mother is ready to dish up. A good stew today she said she would be making, and for pudding, rhubarb and custard.
TEACHER	Well, in that family it was Mother who stayed out of the shop and did all the cooking. Now, finally, let us look at the working class family

Questions

1. What time of day was it in the grocer's shop?
2. Who did all the cooking?
3. How much tea did Mrs Smith buy each week? On which day?
4. What were they going to have for dinner?

Scene 7

CAST

MRS JONES
SID JONES, her husband
APRIL JONES, their daughter
LEN JONES, their son
LIZZIE JONES, their daughter

| MRS JONES | Lizzie, you good for nothing. What did I tell you? Sweep that floor properly, right into the corners. |
| LIZZIE | But Mum, I'm tired. I was working in the bakery at four this morning. |

45

MRS JONES	So I should think. And you keep that job, my girl. You know we need the money.
LIZZIE	Why can't April do it? Why is she allowed to read instead of working?
MRS JONES	You know very well. Your sister is clever. One day she'll go to college and be a teacher.
APRIL	Perhaps, Lizzie, if you worked at school you could read as well.
LIZZIE	Oh, shut up.
MRS JONES	Here's your Da and Len home from the factory. They'll want their tea, so be quiet, Lizzie, you'd better not let them hear you moaning.
SID	Home at last. Starving. Where's me tea, woman?
LEN	Hallo, Ma. I'm going to the darts match tonight at the pub. Can I have me tea soon?
TEACHER	Poor Mrs Jones. Not much time to herself with a family like that. But now you have some idea of how different Victorian families lived.
CHILD	More questions, Miss?
TEACHER	Just a few. I want to know if you have really been listening.
CHILD	We have, Miss. Honest.
TEACHER	We'll see, won't we?

Questions

1. Where did Lizzie work? At what time was she working?
2. Lizzie asks, 'Why can't April do it?' In your own words explain why.
3. Where was Len going after his tea?
4. Where did Len and his father go to work?

Follow-up Work

The questions below cover all the scenes that have been read by the children and may supersede the 'after scene' questions. They may, if the teacher so wishes, be used instead of the after scene questions, or as well as, or dispensed with altogether. They are there to use if they are thought appropriate to the children in the class.

1. Find the following places on your map:
   a) Southampton
   b) The Isle of Wight
   c) Cowes
   d) Brighton
   e) Balmoral
   f) Bristol
2. Where were Queen Victoria and Prince Albert in the first scene?
3. Which places did Prince Albert suggest for their home?
4. Where did the Queen want to live?
5. What did they call their home there?
6. What was the nearest town to it?
7. What did the Queen and her daughters like to do?
8. What was the Swiss Cottage?
9. In the mines, how many hours did the men think they should work?
10. What were the main changes created by Lord Shaftesbury to the lives of the children.
11. Why was it worse for the children in the mines than in the factory?
12. What job did the littlest girl do in the mine?
13. What did the young ladies in scene 3 wish for?
14. Can you remember the name of the man who built an iron bridge?
15. What else did he build?

16. What was its name?
17. Where was it berthed?

The scenes in The Victorians can be used consecutively, or as separate areas of study. The follow-up questions are suggestions that the teacher can use or discard in favour of her/his own ideas.

Research Sources

Victoria and Albert at Home by Tyler Whittle (Routledge and Kegan Paul)
Lord Shaftesbury and Social-Industrial Progress by J. Wesley Bready (George Allen and Unwin)
Victorian Family Life by Jane Shuter (Heinemann)
Victorians (Making History) by Ann Kramer (Franklin Watts)
Victorians (Eyewitness) by Ann Kramer (Dorling Kindersley)

THE ANCIENT GREEKS

A play in three scenes with 26 speaking parts plus extras

When the children have settled down in the classroom, the teacher tells them that they are going to be studying some of the history of the ancient Greeks, people who lived in Greece from about 2,000 to 30 years BC. She tells them it can only be some, because Greek history lasted hundreds of years and covers many aspects of learning, for example, the theatre and drama, scientific discoveries, games and sport, sculpture and art, medicine, wisdom and scholars, politics and ways of governing. But for now, she is beginning about 2,500 years ago, 500 years before Christ was born.

Suggested PROPS

Scene 1 Clip board for the guide and for each child and pencils. Handbags for the ladies. Sun hats for men and women.
Scene 2 A chair for the patient.
Scene 3 Table, grapes, carafe of wine. Dice for the children.

The play

Scene 1

CAST

GUIDE
WINSTON PATEL
MR PATEL
MRS PATEL
MARIAN ROBINSON
MR ROBINSON
MRS ROBINSON

At the theatre of Epidaurus in Greece, tourists, headed by a guide, stand in a group.

GUIDE   Now here we are, standing at the centre of the stage of the theatre of Epidaurus. Look around you and you will see that on the hillsides surrounding us are stone seats arranged in a semi circle. This is where the audience would have been seated to watch the plays and where today many people come to watch plays that are still performed. In the beginning the audience would have sat on the ground, but

	gradually bench-like seats were formed for greater comfort. The actors were here in the central place.
WINSTON	But if the actors were down here, how could they be heard by everyone? They didn't have microphones, did they?
GUIDE	(*laughs*) No, they didn't. But that's a good question. Part of the stories were told by the chorus, a group of people who used music and dance and speaking together, so that they could be heard and understood.
MARIAN	But weren't there any proper actors?
GUIDE	Oh yes, and they would stand in the middle of this space and, so that people knew who they were, they wore masks which they would change from comic to sad as the play demanded. You've probably seen replicas of those masks outside theatres, or on programmes.
WINSTON	Yes, I have. The drama teacher put them on the programme for our school play.
GUIDE	Good. Now you will know why, won't you?
WINSTON	Yes. But what else did the actors do, apart from wearing masks?
GUIDE	Sometimes they would build up their shoes to make themselves appear taller, or wear strange costumes, or they would build a little platform in the centre of the stage to make a leading actor stand out.
MRS PATEL	Were these all actors, or were there actresses as well?
GUIDE	Women were not allowed to take part ... in fact they were not allowed even to go to see the plays.
MR ROBINSON	No women's lib then.

51

GUIDE	No, I'm afraid not.
WINSTON	What about games? Did they play football?
GUIDE	No. Football hadn't been invented then.
MR PATEL	How often were these theatres used?
GUIDE	Once a year there was a big festival of plays, to celebrate the feast of Dionysus, one of their gods. The festival would last three days and people would come and watch all the plays as well as having fun, eating and drinking wine, and probably getting very merry.
MRS ROBINSON	It sounds to me as if they were as bad as we are today.
GUIDE	Well, I suppose some things don't change much.
MARIAN	But I've been thinking. If the actors were down here, they couldn't have had scenery, could they?
GUIDE	Well, not as we know it today, but if you think of their theatre like the shape of a horse-shoe, then at the two ends there would be a kind of building on a higher level with steps down for the actors' and chorus' entrances. The building would also be used as a background and a place to conceal the dressing rooms, and such pieces of equipment or properties needed by the actors. There would also be the stage machinery such as a kind of crane which was used when a god had to appear in a play. It would appear as if he came from heaven or somewhere other than earth. All this was hidden by a kind of arch and because it was in front of what we would call the 'scenery' it was called the 'proscene'. For many theatres today we have a similar construction, which we call 'the proscenium arch'.
MARIAN	What were the plays about?

52

GUIDE	In the beginning they were about myths, old stories about their gods; stories which everyone knew, which helped them to understand what was going on. But then they developed further into comedies about everyday life, making fun of their politicians and so on, or tragedies about the anger of their gods. And this would be a time when they would use the masks. A smiling face for comedy, and a miserable face for tragedy.
MRS ROBINSON	Did they have many gods?
GUIDE	Oh yes. One god, called Thespis, was the god of drama and surprisingly he is remembered even today, because actors are sometimes called thespians. There were many others. One who was king of all the gods was called Zeus. He had a brother called Poseidon who was king of the ocean. Another called Hades was god of the underworld. There were also goddesses and one of the most well known today was Aphrodite, the goddess of love and beauty. That's a lot for you to learn.
TEACHER	That's true. You do have a lot to learn.
CHILD	I shall remember the gods.
CHILD	You'll be god of the underworld because you're low.
CHILD	I shall be the king of the gods.
CHILD	You would. Always thinking you're the best. He's a big-head, isn't he, Miss?
TEACHER	I don't think I'm going to answer that. But do we have any goddesses?
CHILD	I shall be one.
CHILD	Which one?
CHILD	Goddess of beauty, of course.

CHILD	Ha ha! I don't think so.
CHILD	I'd like to go to the festival and have lots to eat and drink. (*He mimes eating and drinking.*)
CHILD	Trust you. You're always thinking of your stomach.
CHILD	But it would be fun, three days' holiday. Would you like it, Miss?
TEACHER	Three days' holiday? From you lot? Great.
CHILDREN	Oh, Miss. You wouldn't like to be without us, would you?
TEACHER	I'm not so sure about that. But you're not so bad, really. Well we'll have to stop now for today. We'll hear some more next time

Scene 2

CAST

PATIENT
DOCTOR 1
DOCTOR 2

A patient is seen slumped in a chair. His head is in his hands and he's moaning a little. After a moment, two doctors enter.

DOCTOR 1	What a noise. What's the matter with you?
PATIENT	Ah, doctor, I am in agony. A dreadful pain in my stomach. Oh.
DOCTOR 1	Poor you. But there, you must have done something very wrong. Your pain shows the gods are angry with you. You must take yourself to one of the temples of Asclepius, god of healing, if you wish to be cured. Make sure when you get there you wash thoroughly and

	make a sacrifice, take a fowl or animal with you for the purpose. You will then spend the night in the temple and hope that Asclepius will tell you in a dream your cure.
DOCTOR 2	No, no. What old-fashioned nonsense! I have become a follower of the great Hippocrates, a doctor who lives on the island of Kos. He teaches that doctors must examine a patient carefully and to find a scientific cause of the illness. He often prescribes herbal medicine and gives a lot of advice about diet and exercise. He made all doctors swear an oath that we would always work to save the life of a patient. It has become known as the Hippocratic Oath, for all doctors to follow. Come patient, come with me and I will examine you and between us we will find a cure for your pain. (*Doctor 2 and patient go off.*)
DOCTOR 1	Hippocrates? Never heard of him. I must follow and see what happens. (*He exits.*)
TEACHER	Now, has anyone heard of the Hippocratic Oath? No? Well, doctors still follow it today. They are duty bound to save life.
CHILD	I'm glad we don't have doctors like the first one.
CHILD	Wouldn't you like to spend a night in a temple?
CHILD	No, I wouldn't, I'd be scared.
CHILD	(*making ghost noises*) Ahhh. Come here, wash yourself and you will be cured.
CHILD	Get off, there's nothing wrong with me.
CHILD	Are you sure? What about your brain?
CHILD	What about yours?
TEACHER	Right, that's enough teasing. Let's get on with the next scene.

Scene 3

CAST

PERSEPHONE
ARIADNE
ATHENA
ADRIANE
NASSIS
SOPHO
LAURA
ARCHIMEDES
MR HERON

A group of women are lying on cushions on the floor, beside a table. The women are eating grapes and talking to each other. Near to them, also on the floor, a group of children are playing knucklebones, a kind of dice made of animal bones.

PERSEPHONE	I'm so bored. The festival is on and all the men are there. Why can't we go?
ARIADNE	You know we can't go. Women aren't allowed anywhere and we're not even allowed to have a say at the Assembly.
ATHENA	Second-class citizens we are.
ADRIANE	There's nothing we can do about it. Remember our friend? She decided to disobey the rules. And we know what happened to her.
ATHENA	Don't talk about it. It gives me the shudders.
ADRIANE	Well, try to forget about it, unless you want to die also.
PERSEPHONE	We have to stay and look after the children. Look at them now, playing. We should be glad they're happy. Is anyone winning the game?

NASSIS	Yes, Sopho. He wins every time.
SOPHO	No I don't. Not every time.
LAURA	I'm tired of playing this game. I keep losing.
ATHENA	That teaches you to try harder so that you can win next time.
NASSIS	I think I'm going to stop playing knucklebones. I'm sure you're cheating, Sopho.
SOPHO	No, I'm not.
LAURA	Well, how do you keep getting them in the right place?
SOPHO	I'm clever, that's how.
LAURA	And conceited with it.
SOPHO	I am not conceited.
NASSIS	You are. You think you're the top of everything.
ADRIANE	Oh don't fight, children. It's far too hot. I know, let's go out to the garden. You can practise your running. Perhaps you could find something you could use as hurdles, too.
CHILDREN	Oh yes, let's go outside.
ATHENA	It won't be long now till the time of the games. Perhaps we shall be able to watch the runner bringing the flame from Athens to signal the start of the great Olympiad.
LAURA	I should like to see that, but I wish I could go to see the games as well.
PERSEPHONE	I'm sure you do, but we can't, so it's no good wishing.
ADRIANE	I would like to take part but I know it's not allowed. Do you think that one day women will be allowed to run and hurdle, and take part in all the games? I suppose I'm stupid even to imagine it, but I'm sure women could compete with men.
ATHENA	Oh, come on, stop day-dreaming, Adriane, we're on our way outside.

(They all go off, to return a few moments later, with two men.)

PERSEPHONE Now, children, let me introduce you to these men. This is Mr Heron the farmer who looks after all the fields, and this is Mr Archimedes, a scientist. I think we had better keep quiet for a while because they are having a discussion. Let us sit over here. *(The women and children move away and sit down.)*

ARCHIMEDES Mr Heron, you are looking very sad. In fact, I have never seen such a long face. Can you tell me what is wrong?

MR HERON Well, everything really. It's the heat, you see; no rain for months. I've tried planting wheat and barley, but as you can see, they simply have not grown, they just shrivel and die. If only I had the means of getting water from the river up to my land. I've tried getting it in pitchers, my slaves have tried various means, but it's no good. The water just sinks into the ground and is dried up in a few minutes. Oh dear what can I do?

ARCHIMEDES I think I might be able to help you there. I have developed a large screw-type piece of equipment which, if used correctly, would do just what you want. It would enable you to bring the water up from the river to irrigate your land.

MR HERON That would be a wonderful thing. Do you mean to say that I could water my crops, without having to carry every little drop in a hand vessel?

ARCHIMEDES I certainly do mean to say. I have been experimenting with this idea for a long time, and I do believe it will work in the way you require. Come, let me show you. I have here an example of my invention. I would like you to see it. Then I will explain it to you more fully. (*They exit.*)

TEACHER I think that's enough for today, children. I hope you have learned something about the Ancient Greeks. Later on there will be some follow up work for you to do and we will learn more about the people in the play.

Questions

1. Could you say what a 'proscenium arch' is? What was it called in ancient Greece?
2. How did the actors show the difference between tragedy and comedy?
3. What were the first plays about?
4. In scene three what game were the children playing?
5. What did the women wish they were allowed to do?

6. Why did Mr Heron, the farmer, look so miserable?
7. What did Archimedes invent? What was it for?
8. What do you understand by the Hippocratic Oath?

Follow-up Work

1. Draw a picture of the masks of tragedy and comedy.
2. Imagine you are a journalist in ancient Greece, and write an article about the people at the drama festival.
3. Find the country of Greece on a map and mark on it the theatre of Epidaurus.
4. To watch all the festival, each person would have to pay five and a half dinarii. If a group of 27 people went to the festival, how much money would it cost?
5. In twos, imagine you are the doctors (1 & 2) in scene two and discuss the healing methods used by both.

Research Sources

The Theatre, An Introduction, Second edition by Oscar G. Brockett (Holt, Rhinehart and Winston)

Legacies From Ancient Greece by Anita Ganeri (Belitha Press)

Myths And Civilizations Of The Ancient Greeks by Hazel Mary Martell (Franklin Watts, Australia)

Ancient Greeks by Clare Chandler (Wayland)

Clothes and Crafts in Ancient Greece by Philip Steele (Zoe Books)

Greek Life by John Guy (Ticktock)

THE ROMANS

A play in seven scenes, 50 speakers including children in class

PROPS: Toys, wedding gear (as described in the text), whip for slave master, a doll bound, rod for hair curling, jewellery.

This section of the book is for the older children in KS2, because there is a lot more reading/narration. If the reading level is good the teacher's role could be shared among the children.

The play has been divided into separate lessons with question and tasks at the end of each although, as always, such questions are optional and will depend on the teacher's wishes.

When the children enter and are seated the teacher tells them that this time they will be learning about the Romans who, like the Vikings, were invaders of Britain.

CHILD	Where did the Romans live, Miss?
TEACHER	In Italy. That was their real country.
CHILD	Why did they want to invade England?
CHILD	I'd much rather stay in Italy. They get much more sun.
CHILD	Yes, and their pasta's good, too.
TEACHER	I'm not sure they ate pasta then. Anyway, it was their Emperor, Julius Caesar, who wanted to add England to his empire.
CHILD	What a cheek. How did he get here then, Miss?
TEACHER	It was in the year 55 BC (that is before Christ was born) that Julius Caesar attempted the first invasion. I want you to imagine that a group of English (Saxon) soldiers are on watch above the cliffs of Dover.

Scene 1

CAST

4 SOLDIERS

SOLDIER 1	Look men, look! Boats coming across the Channel. What do you make of it?
SOLDIER 2	I don't like this. I can't see all that clearly, there's such a sea mist, but there seems to be a huge fleet.
SOLDIER 3	They are about to invade. Come on men. We must stop them. This way. We'll start by making such a noise that in the mist they won't know how many of us there are.
SOLDIER 4	He's right. Come on, men. YELL AS LOUD AS YOU CAN.

TEACHER	And that's what they did.
CHILD	So then what happened?
TEACHER	Well, Caesar had landed on the beach but when he saw and heard how the English soldiers responded –
CAESAR	Back to your boats, men. They've seen us. Turn north-east along the coast. We'll find a better place to catch them unawares.
CHILD	Then where did they go?
TEACHER	They landed on the coast of Kent between Walmer and Deal. And that began 400 years of Roman occupation.
CHILD	If they lived in Italy, why do we call them Romans and not Italians?
TEACHER	That's a good question. Well, all those years ago Italy was divided into tribes, rather than one whole country, so listen to two mothers

63

telling their children of a legend about how Rome was founded.
(*The class sits round two pupils already cast as the mothers and others as the children.*)

Scene 2

CAST

2 MOTHERS
CHILDREN

MOTHER 1	Now, children, listen carefully. I'm going to tell you the story of two brothers who were the founders of our beautiful city, Rome.
CHILD	What were their names, Mother?
MOTHER 2	Quiet, child. You will be told in a moment.
CHILD	I'm sorry.
MOTHER 1	Apology accepted. Now, the brothers' names were Romulus and Remus. They were abandoned at birth, and a she-wolf found them and looked after them.
MOTHER 2	She fed them as if they were her cubs.
MOTHER 1	Yes she did, and they grew and were healthy boys. But when they were too big for the wolf, they left her and eventually they were found by a shepherd and his wife, who looked after them until they were grown up. Then the brothers left the shepherd and his wife and made their way to the city which they called Rome and declared themselves its founders.
CHILD	What happened then?
MOTHER 2	Well, something really rather terrible. The brothers had a dreadful quarrel about who should rule the city and sad to say, Romulus

won and, so that Remus would never question him, Romulus murdered Remus. So Romulus was the Emperor, the supreme head of Rome.

Questions *(to be answered in writing)*

1. Where, in England, did Julius Caesar first try to land?
2. Where did he finally land?
3. How was Rome founded?

TEACHER   I hope you remember what happened in lesson one. I'll just remind you. The two mothers were telling the children about Rome and they had reached the point when Romulus had murdered his brother Remus and became Supreme Emperor of Rome. One of you asked, was he punished? Does anyone remember why he wasn't?

CHILD   Because he was the Emperor and couldn't be punished.

TEACHER   Good. Now we'll continue with the rest of the story.

CHILD   So, he got away with it.
MOTHER 2   I'm afraid he did.
CHILD   But then what?
MOTHER 1   It was rather strange, but at this time there were no women in Rome.
CHILD   What did they do without women?
MOTHER 2   They tried to persuade another tribe to send them some of their women. When they refused, the Romans kidnapped some from the Sabine tribe. This caused them to start a war, which continued until the women persuaded the men to make peace.

CHILD	So the men did what the women told them to do. Did they always?
TEACHER	No they did not. In fact, women were second-class citizens. A woman couldn't inherit her husband's money, nor could she divorce him, though he could divorce her.
CHILD	That's not fair.
TEACHER	No, it wasn't and even worse, women, as well as men, were sold as slaves. They would stand in the marketplace with a label round their neck, telling people their particular skills, for example, cook or dressmaker or gardener, and the men would come and look them over and buy them.
CHILD	Did everyone have slaves?
TEACHER	Everyone but the very poor. The really rich Roman might have one hundred slaves and a noble perhaps as many as ten thousand working on his land.
CHILD	I think the idea of slaves is horrid.
TEACHER	So do we all today. But then – well, listen to the next scene as we find out what happened in the Roman slave market.

Questions

1. What was strange about the population of Rome at that time?
2. How did the Romans try to overcome the problem?

Scene 3

CAST

3 ROMANS
4 WOMEN
1 SLAVE MASTER

ROMAN 1	Not many slaves to be had today.
ROMAN 2	A miserable lot, I'd say. How many are you after?
ROMAN 3	Only one today. A good-looking cook would do.
ROMAN 1	Must be good-looking, eh?
ROMAN 3	Yes. I can't stand ugly women. What about you two?

ROMAN 2	I could do with several.
ROMAN 1	Depends on what I can get.
ROMAN 2	Right. Let's move over there and observe them. You can tell a lot about women when they're not sure they're being looked at. (*As the men move away, the women start talking.*)
WOMAN 1	Not much to look at, are they?
WOMAN 2	One of them isn't bad.
WOMAN 3	Well, whoever buys me, I shan't care as long as he treats me well.
WOMAN 4	Most of them are fair.
WOMAN 2	Yes, but some beat you.
WOMAN 1	Oh don't.
WOMAN 3	Well, I can cook anything they ask for as long as they leave me alone to get on with it.
WOMAN 4	I hope his wife is young with a good figure, if I'm to make dresses for her. The fat ones are so much more difficult to make clothes for. (*She pretends to be fat and the others laugh.*)
SLAVE MASTER	Talking? Laughing? You'd better stop that or you'll feel my whip across your backs. No Roman will buy a chattering woman. (*The women back away and are silent as the men come forward.*)
ROMAN 3	(*Pointing to the third woman*) I'll take that one. Twenty-five sesterius, you said?
SLAVE MASTER	That's right, sir, twenty-five sesterius.
ROMAN 2	I'll take the dressmaker and the gardener. Fifty sesterius.
SLAVE MASTER	Thank you, sir.
ROMAN 1	I'll take the rest. There you are, my sesterius.

SLAVE MASTER	(*counts the money*) Just right, sir. (*To the women*) Come on now, you good-for-nothings. Follow your owners.
CHILD	Why were the women treated so badly?
TEACHER	It's difficult to understand. The Romans adored their babies and they wouldn't have had those without a woman, so you'd think they would at least respect them.
CHILD	Did the fathers look after the babies?
TEACHER	No, if they were well off they would have slaves to look after them. But they had strange ideas about babies. They believed that their whole bodies should be bound with cloth to make their limbs grow straight. The right hand would be unbound to make sure that they grew up right-handed because to be left-handed was unlucky.
CHILD	But if the slaves looked after the babies, what did the mothers do?
TEACHER	Listen now to a mother talking to another slave.

Scene 4

CAST

MOTHER
SLAVE

MOTHER   Come here, slave. While my baby is being
                looked after by one of your friends, it is your
                job to look after my clothes, keep my hair in
                good condition and style it as I wish. When
                I wish to go to the baths, you are to put out
                my clothes. If I am going to a social gathering,
                you must make sure that the right garments
                are made ready. You will also be expected to
                make me a new gown when I need one and
                of course all must be washed frequently. And
                I must have my perfume at the baths. If I have
                cause to complain, you will be beaten. Is that
                clear?

SLAVE   Yes, madam.

Questions

1. In the slave market, how did the Roman men know what
   the women could do?
2. Name the tasks the mother of the baby tells the slave girl
   to do.
3. Ask your music teacher to find some music for you and
   choreograph a dance for a slave girl.

TEACHER	That mother was one of the rich ones. The poor mothers did not have slaves, so they looked after the children themselves.
CHILD	Did the children go to school?
TEACHER	Yes, most of them. Elementary schools focused on basic reading, writing and arithmetic. The teacher was often an ex-slave or disabled ex-soldier. Elementary school teachers had very little pay, and people did not respect them. Classes were small, about twelve pupils. Lessons were given in the open air or in a hired room, sometimes at the back of a shop. There was a chair for the teacher and benches for the children. Wealthy children were educated at home and if the family was active in politics the children had to learn both Latin and Greek. The third stage of education was public speaking, known as rhetoric. Very rich families might send their sons to Athens or Crete to study under famous Greek teachers. The great Roman lawyer Cicero was a student until he was thirty years of age. Public speaking was essential for those who wanted to be lawyers or politicians.
CHILD	Did the children have toys, Miss?
TEACHER	Oh yes, lots of them. The babies had rattles and dolls. Later they had hobby horses, toy chariots, metal hoops and wooden wheels to bowl along. A rich child might have a chariot big enough to be pulled by a goat or a pair of geese. Some also had little carts drawn by mice which were raced against each other. Marbles were made from glass and pottery. Country children used hazelnuts or walnuts. Other children had whips and tops, kites,

swings, see-saws and go-karts. Bigger boys fenced with wooden swords. Ball games were popular (even with grown women). Sport, wrestling, boxing, riding (no stirrups, they hadn't been invented) and chariot racing. Children also had to help at home, keeping the fire going, gathering firewood, nuts, berries and mushrooms.

CHILD   That kept them busy. Weren't they lucky to have so many toys? But racing with mice. Oh, Miss!

TEACHER   Well, that's what the books tell us.

CHILD   Did the children have pets?

TEACHER   We know they had dogs not just as pets but as rat catchers or guard dogs. They often called them Celer (meaning swift) or Ferox (meaning fierce).

Questions

1. Name four toys the children had.
2. Choose one out of all the toys and write a short piece about how you imagine the children played with it.

TEACHER   In the last scene we learned about the children's schooling, their toys and their pets. But let us leave the children for now and go back to the women. First I want to tell you about a wedding. Normally women wore clothes with a simple cut, in bright colours for the rich, dull for the poor. They wore a long tunic with short or no sleeves, called a stola. Over that a rectangle of cloth called a palla. Wealthy women imported silk from India or China, but poor women made do with coarse cloth. Cotton, which came from

India or Sudan, was rare. They wore leather or wooden sandals, and slippers with cork soles. But the wedding dress was very different. Let us imagine that we are in the home of a Roman family and the wedding is on this very day. The mother is talking to the bride.

Scene 5

CAST

MOTHER
BRIDE
SON-IN-LAW
MARRIED WOMAN

MOTHER	Now you know what will happen. Today is a most important day in your life, for it is your wedding day. I hope you slept well in your wedding dress. It's not too tight so you should have done. Now I have to tie a woollen belt around you and make sure the knot can only be undone by your future husband. There, is that comfortable?
BRIDE	A bit tight but I suppose it will do. I daren't eat anything.
MOTHER	Well, it's not for long so you can put up with it, can't you?
BRIDE	Yes. Now, my veil. It's a beautiful colour.
MOTHER	Yes, I'm glad it has to be orange. The colour suits you. Now let me first do your hair. The curling iron is hot so hold still until I have finished. Six ringlets then the veil. Cover your face, and then let me put the crown of flowers on the top. There, that's beautiful. What about

73

your gold necklace and bracelet? Here they are. Put them on. And last, the yellow shoes to bring you good luck and babies. Ah, I long for those, my grandchildren.

BRIDE   I'm not so sure. I'd like a little time first. But I know it is in the hands of the gods. Oh, here is my husband to be, and the married lady who will pronounce us married.

MOTHER   Yes, go to greet them. Oh, you look so lovely together. Greetings son-in-law to be.

SON-IN-LAW   Greetings (*he bows*). Now let us begin. If you, Madam, would take our hands –

MARRIED WOMAN   Of course. Now give me your right hand, each of you, and I will join them together. So. Now I pronounce you married.

SON-IN-LAW   I thank you.

MARRIED WOMAN   I have enjoyed meeting you and the little task I have done for you. (*They exit.*)

CHILD   And that was all? A wedding like that?

TEACHER   Yes, that was all.

CHILD   Funny idea. And, an orange veil. Horrid, I think.

TEACHER   Well, we're used to seeing white veils, so orange does seem strange to us.

CHILD   The women seem nicer than the men. Were they?

TEACHER   Well, yes, most of them, but some women were feared by the Romans and some were downright dangerous. Take Boudicca, or Boadicea as we call her, who led a great and terrifying revolt in Britain. Cleopatra, who was considered so beautiful, tempted two great men, Julius Caesar and Mark Anthony.

In the end, both women committed suicide because they probably realised that eventually

74

they would lose their lives at the hands of an angry Roman.

Now, in order to learn about another woman from Roman times, listen to a conversation between the Emperor Claudius and his third wife Messalina.

Question

In pairs, imagine one of you is the mother and the other the bride. Using the instructions in the script, talk the bride through the wedding preparations.

TEACHER
: In the last lesson, we heard about a wedding and how different it was, and we began talking about a rather unpleasant woman, Messalina, then third wife of the Emperor Claudius. I hope you remember.

CHILDREN
: Yes, Miss.

TEACHER
: Good. Now, let us continue.

Scene 6

CAST

CLAUDIUS
MESSALINA
BRUTUS
SLAVE

MESSALINA
: Claudius, my love. Have I your assurance that my wishes are your command?

CLAUDIUS
: You know that is so. Just say what you want and it shall be yours.

MESSALINA	I knew that would be your reply, dear husband.
CLAUDIUS	So, tell me what it is you want.
MESSALINA	Later, later, I must be ready for my hairdresser. Until later. (*She goes.*)
	(*Messalina enters another room. A slave appears and bows.*)
SLAVE	My lady Empress. Your wish?
MESSALINA	Yes. Fetch Senator Marcus at once.
SLAVE	Certainly, Highness. (*He exits.*)
	(*Messalina paces the room angrily. The slave returns with the Senator.*)
SENATOR	(*bowing*) Highness.
MESSALINA	(*to the servant*) Leave us.
	(*Slave exits backwards*)
MESSALINA	Now, have you thought about my proposal? Are you agreed?
MARCUS	Madam, my dear, it is not possible. As I told you before. On my life I cannot agree to your request.
MESSALINA	Cannot or will not?
MARCUS	Dear lady, you make it so difficult for me. If only I could agree, I would gladly...
MESSALINA	Coward. You are afraid of shadows. Do you not know that I would make sure that Claudius never found out. Has not our love affair convinced you of my ability to dissemble?
MARCUS	It has and I know that I am first in your heart, but still I say, with great sadness, I cannot do as you ask.
MESSALINA	Very well, leave me now. I must think.
MARCUS	As you wish, my dear. Until we meet again.
	(*Marcus leaves the room and after a moment Messalina walks towards the exit.*)
MESSALINA	Slave, find the Emperor. Bring him to me.
CLAUDIUS	Messalina. Dear one. What can be the matter?

	I heard you calling and you sounded so fraught. What has upset you?
MESSALINA	I'll tell you what has upset me. Marcus, one of the senators. He refused to obey my will. Trivial, perhaps, but not only did he refuse, but with such disrespect, rudeness of an appalling kind, to me, the great Empress.
CLAUDIUS	Rudeness? Disrespect? He will know my displeasure, nay, my anger. How dare he? (*He calls*) Slave!
SLAVE	You called, Highness?
CLAUDIUS	Yes, find Senator Marcus and take him to the prison house and there lock him up.
SLAVE	And if he asks why?
CLAUDIUS	It is my command, you imbecile. Go. (*Slave exits backwards.*)
MESSALINA	Thank you, my dear husband. I will now, at last, go to my hairdresser. (*She exits.*)
CLAUDIUS	(*Sits and thinks for a while. Then he turns as a man comes into the room. Claudius greets him.*) Why, Brutus, my friend, what brings you here?
BRUTUS	A difficult mission, I fear.
CLAUDIUS	Difficult? Well, come on, tell me.
BRUTUS	I have just been informed that you have sent Marcus to the prison house. May I ask why?
CLAUDIUS	He is a traitor. He has refused a request from Messalina, my beloved wife. Has been disrespectful, rude even.
BRUTUS	And did she tell you the request?
CLAUDIUS	No. It was probably none of my business, some woman's thing I believe.
BRUTUS	Dear friend, I'm afraid you are wrong, unless you call an affair with one of the senators a woman's thing.
CLAUDIUS	Affair? With one of the senators? But you

	don't, you can't mean my wife, Messalina? An affair? With the Senator? No, I will not believe it.
BRUTUS	I'm afraid you must know it to be true. And how I hate to be the bearer of such bad news.
CLAUDIUS	Go on man.
BRUTUS	You remember your absence some months ago? When you were on duty bound from the Senate?
CLAUDIUS	Yes, yes, what of it?
BRUTUS	It is common knowledge that your wife married another during your time away.
CLAUDIUS	(*explodes*) What? This is treason. She couldn't have. Take care what you say.
BRUTUS	It is true. The marriage is recorded.
CLAUDIUS	Then she must die. Find her. Take her to the prison house with her lover and her new husband. They must die. Now, leave me.
TEACHER	Now, that was rather dramatic, wasn't it?
CHILD	She must have been a bad woman to marry again while she still had a husband.
TEACHER	She was. And then poor Claudius married again after Messalina died. He married a woman called Agrippina, one who apparently was power mad. She persuaded Claudius to adopt her son so that he would be the next Emperor and when, in AD 54, Claudius died of a mysterious illness, it was wondered if Agrippina was responsible.
CHILD	Was she?
TEACHER	No one ever found out. But now you can hear about one of the women who wasn't bad. Her name was Hortensia, and she helped women to fight for their rights. A sort of early women's lib campaigner. The Roman Senate put a tax

on one thousand four hundred rich women in order to pay for the current war. Hortensia fought this because she said that women should not have to pay for a war that was the responsibility of the men. The men backed down and taxed only the very richest four hundred.

CHILD   Good for her.

CHILD   But I bet the four hundred weren't pleased.

TEACHER   No, I don't suppose they were. But now, we have talked a lot about the women so let us consider the men.

Question

Why was Claudius so angry with his wife Messalina? Write a poem about this, as your answer.

CHILD   You said we would learn about the men, Miss.

TEACHER   And so you shall.

CHILD   What did they do?

TEACHER   Most men joined the army, at first as part-timers, rather like our Territorial Army. The Roman army was divided into huge groups called legions. A legion could hold up to six thousand soldiers. As the Empire grew (more countries were conquered) the soldiers had to become full time and that meant they had to serve for twenty-five years. The best trained, equipped and paid soldier was the legionary, who had to be a citizen of Rome, or the son of one. Other soldiers, who were recruited from places the legionaries had defeated in battle, were not pure Roman. They were called auxiliaries and they were often very badly treated. When there was no battle to fight, the soldiers had to use their engineering skills to build camps, forts, bridges, roads and walls. The most famous road, which still exists in England in part, is called Fosse Way. Like all Roman roads it was made in a perfectly straight line. But listen to these soldiers at work on a well known wall. Hadrian's Wall, built by the order of the Emperor Hadrian and begun in AD 122.

Scene 7

CAST

6 LEGIONARIES
SEVERAL NON-SPEAKING AUXILIARIES

LEGION 1	Come on you auxiliaries. Don't pretend you're Roman. You came from nowhere, dogs, beasts. You'd better get on or you'll get the beating you deserve.
LEGION 2	Why wait? They're all bound to be kicked or beaten some time during the day. That'll make them work faster.
LEGION 3	Oh come on, don't waste time with the rats. We've got to get on with the wall. If it's not completed we'll have the northern tribes coming to attack us.
LEGION 4	That's true and we don't want to waste time mowing down those barbarians. Anyway a battle would cause a delay. Come on, dogs, get a move on.
LEGION 5	Not much of a delay as long as we send these rats in before us. Let them be disposed of first,

	then we can finish off the intruders. (*Laughter*) Then we can get the next fort along the wall built.
LEGION 6	You mean Housesteads? Yeah, that's important. The first latrine block. About time too. But we're supposed to connect the furnace and hypocaust system. Very clever, to channel hot water from a furnace below a room along pipes where it is needed.
LEGION 1	Do you think we can instruct this brainless lot in heating?
LEGION 2	I doubt it. But it's got to be done.
LEGION 3	Perhaps they can learn to light the furnace while we do the channelling.
LEGION 4	They can dig the ditches for the pipes.
LEGION 5	And maybe construct the pillars holding the roof of the hot air system.
LEGION 6	I think you're being optimistic. But perhaps they'll learn if we beat them hard enough.
TEACHER	Not a very charming group, were they? They were cruel to the auxiliaries but they were also cruel in other ways. For example, they loved gladiator fighting. In the great Colosseum or the Circus Maximus in Rome, famous tournaments would be arranged with the gladiators fighting sometimes slaves or wild beasts, lions, tigers. There was always a nasty death, mostly the slaves, sometimes the gladiator, sometimes the animal. In those days, I'm afraid they held life very lightly.

Romans, particularly senators, are usually pictured wearing the toga but because it is such a complicated garment it was kept for special occasions. Normally they wore a simple tunic. Like the women, the men loved jewellery, gold particularly, which was very expensive and could only be afforded by the wealthy. Poorer men and women had to make do with bronze. Men also occasionally wore make up.

The Roman Empire was powerful while it was growing but defending the frontier was very hard and by AD 476 it had broken up.

The Eastern Empire, based around Constantinople (now Istanbul in Turkey) survived until the fifteenth century. But the once mighty Western Empire lay in ruins.

Questions

1. How many men were in a legion?
2. What was a hypocaust?

Further questions and tasks for the pupils

1. If a Roman noble wanted 100 slaves at 25 sesterius each, how much would he have to pay?
2. Which of the scenes in the play did you like the most?
3. Choose a partner and have a discussion on the scenes.

Research Sources

Roman Britain; Life in an Imperial Province by Keith Branigan (Reader's Digest)
Ancient Roman Women by Brian Williams (Heinemann)
The Romans by Peter Hicks (Wayland)
Ancient Roman Children by Richard Tames (Heinemann)

THE TIME OF THE TUDORS

When the children have come in and settled down, the teacher tells them that they will be studying the Tudors. The children ask questions.

CHILD   What are the Tudors, Miss?

TEACHER   Tudor was the surname of the Royal family a long time ago. Our Royal family's name is Windsor and before the Tudors it was Plantagenet.

CHILD   So when did they reign, Miss?

TEACHER   Well, the first Tudor king was Henry VII, who, it is reported, took the crown from the Plantagenet King Richard III at the Battle of Bosworth Field, in 1485.

CHILD   So he wasn't a relation then, was he?

TEACHER   No, but he reckoned he was the rightful king then.

CHILD   Did the people like the king?

TEACHER   Perhaps it would be a good idea for you to hear what people said. Listen.

Scene 1 *The views of the people*

CAST

BELINDA
KATE
MARY
DAVID
JOHN

JOHN   So we've got a new king now.

KATE   How did that happen?

DAVID   'Tis said he took the crown at the battle.

MARY   What battle?

BELINDA   Bosworth of course. Don't you listen to folk talking?

MARY   Why should I?

JOHN   If you did you'd know a bit more. I heard he's called Henry. He'll be the VII.

KATE   Do you reckon he'll be better than Richard?

BELINDA   Better looking 'tis said. Let's hope he makes a better king as well.

KATE   Anyway, we're a bit behind. He's married now

	to a lady called Elizabeth and they've got a baby son called Arthur.
DAVID	News doesn't come to us in the village very quickly. How old is the baby?
KATE	I don't know, but I heard that the King didn't marry as soon as he was crowned.
JOHN	And he made his wife wait for her coronation.
BELINDA	I shouldn't think that pleased her.
JOHN	No, a lot of people were very annoyed with him.
KATE	What's he like? I mean, is he a good man?
DAVID	I did hear it said that he is cold, unfriendly and will do anything for money.
MARY	Let's hope he's better than Richard. Anyway, we'll never see him. The court's too far away from us. Well, I'm going. Potatoes to dig.
BELINDA	And cows to milk. God be with you.
KATE	Eggs to collect. Goodbye.
	(*They all go off.*)
CHILD	What happened then, Miss?
TEACHER	Later on, Elizabeth had another boy and he was called Henry, after his father. But now, let's get on to the time when Arthur, who had been given the title Prince of Wales, and Henry were grown up. Arthur married a girl called Catherine of Aragon. But, the following year Arthur died, and seven years later Henry VII also died, which meant that Prince Henry became Henry VIII, and, wishing to marry and have an heir, married Catherine, Arthur's widow. But after a number of years together, he decided he was fed up with Catherine and wanted the marriage ended. He had also fallen in love with someone else, Anne Boleyn, who

was a lady-in-waiting at court. He asked the Pope, with whom he was on good terms (the Pope had already given him the title of Defender of the Faith) to allow the end of the marriage, but the Pope would not agree. Henry was angry and called Cardinal Wolsey, a close friend, to help him persuade the Pope. Now, listen and you will understand.

Scene 2

CAST

HENRY VII
CARDINAL WOLSEY

HENRY   Wolsey, listen to me. Apart from the fact that I can no longer stand the sight of that silly Catherine, my wife, who has given me a daughter, Mary, instead of the male heir I crave, I have met and fallen in love with a younger, wonderful lady, called Anne. And I wish to be married to her. You are to persuade the Holy Father that my marriage must be ended.

WOLSEY   But Sire, you are the King. Your people would not take kindly to their king having a divorce.

HENRY   You're too scared of the people, Wolsey. As you say I am the King and the people should not criticise what I do. But listen. I have lain awake at night worrying about my marriage to Catherine. She is my brother's widow. Isn't it unlawful? To marry a sister-in-law? Am I not committing a sin? The Pope must agree. Go to him, Wolsey, and put the matter to him. Go. Now. (*Wolsey bows himself out.*)

HENRY
(*to himself*) Little does he know that I have already married my beautiful Anne Boleyn. What a thing I have done. The Holy Father will forgive me, I am sure, and agree to the end of my hateful marriage to Catherine. (*He goes out.*)

TEACHER
Well, he really has been rather wicked, hasn't he? But now listen again to what happens when the Cardinal returns.

Scene 3

CAST

HENRY VIII
CARDINAL WOLSEY
CARDINAL CAMPEGGIO

HENRY
So you have returned. With good news, I am sure. What? A long face? Don't tell me you have failed?

WOLSEY
Sire, the Holy Father refused.

HENRY
What? Refused? (*To Campeggio*) Who are you?

CAMPEGGIO
I am Cardinal Campeggio from Rome, Sire. The Holy Father has ordered that the matter must be decided in a court of law. And I have been sent to oversee the problem of the end of the marriage.

HENRY
Stuff and nonsense. A court of law. But whatever happens, I shall break away from the Catholic Church. I will not be dictated to, even by the Pope. I shall create my own church and I shall call it The Church of England. I'll pay no more service to the papists. We shall be Protestants.

CARDINALS (*together, horrified*) But Sire.

HENRY Enough. It shall be so, and the country is to be told they must follow ... I am now going to return to my dear Anne. She is expecting our first child. Pray God it will be a son, my heir. (*He goes off chuckling.*)

TEACHER Later on, in May 1533, the court of law, this time under another man, a Bishop Cranmer, declared Henry's marriage to Catherine ended and his marriage to Anne legal. But Henry was again disappointed. The baby Anne was expecting turned out to be another girl. She was called Elizabeth and although Henry was proud of both his daughters – particularly Mary, who was clever at languages, science and music – he dearly wanted a son. Even so, when Mary was only nine years of age, he gave her her own court at Ludlow Castle and she was called the Princess of Wales. Yet the longing for a son to be his heir never left him. Anne had recently given birth to a son who had died and anyway, by this time he was as tired of Anne as he had been of Catherine. So he put about evil stories of her and her brother and they were arrested and later executed, as were her father and three other men who had befriended her. Before her execution, Anne wrote a letter.

ANNE Good Christian people, I am come hither to die, for according to the law and by the law I am judged to die, and I will speak nothing against it. I am come hither to accuse no man, nor to speak anything of that, whereof I am and condemned to die, but I pray God save the King and send him long to reign over you.

for a gentler prince was there never; and to me he was a good gentle and sovereign lord, and if any person will merit cause I require them to judge the best. And thus I take my leave of the world and you all and I heartily desire you to pray for me. O Lord have mercy on me, to God I commend my soul.

TEACHER	That was brave of her, wasn't it?
CHILD	How could she say Henry was kind when she knew he had sentenced her to death?
TEACHER	Hard to believe, isn't it? But now, let us hear Henry again talking to another wife-to-be.

Scene 4

CAST

HENRY VIII
JANE SEYMOUR

HENRY	Come, my little love. Now with that silly cat Anne dead, we can live our lives together.
JANE	I can hardly believe it. From the time we met I knew we would one day marry, yet there was Anne.
HENRY	Forget her. We will be married tomorrow. She has been dead for ten days. She is forgotten. Come, let us to the church and arrange the marriage. *(They go off.)*
CHILD	Ten days? He was an awful man.
CHILD	Yes, to have one wife killed and straight away marry again.

91

TEACHER   You are right. Of course even a king couldn't do anything like that now. But he did and a few months later he got his wish. Jane had a baby boy, and there was great celebrating in the streets. The baby was called Prince Edward and, because at last he had an heir, Henry sent his daughters away, telling them they no longer had any claim on the throne. But unhappily, Jane died two weeks later, and to his sorrow, it became clear that Edward wasn't strong in health and would probably die young. So Henry had to marry again, to try for another son. He spoke to Cromwell, a senior minister.

Scene 5

CAST

HENRY VIII
CROMWELL
HOLBEIN, an artist

CROMWELL   You sent for me, Sire?
HENRY   Yes. Now I have a problem. Since the death of my dear wife Jane, I have realised that I must marry once more. Edward is not strong and it is essential that I have a healthy son, I need your help to find a wife for me. (*Cromwell thinks.*)
HENRY   Come on, man. I need an answer. Hurry up.
CROMWELL   My apologies, Sire, I was thinking. I do have news of a German Princess of, I am told, great beauty. I believe she would be entirely suitable for your Highness.
HENRY   A great beauty, eh? Well, send her to me. At

once! For I have to marry again; an heir I must have. I firmly believed that my dear Jane would give me a healthy son, but it wasn't to be and poor Edward is a delicate and sickly lad, who, God save us, may not live to be king in my place. So hurry, go to her family and bring me back her likeness. GO!

CROMWELL   At once, as you say, Sire.

TEACHER   And so Henry had to wait until Cromwell returned with Mr Holbein, an artist, to show the picture of the German Princess, Anne of Cleves. When Henry saw the picture he was enchanted and with great excitement said:

HENRY   Wonderful. You are right. She is a great beauty. Bring her to me with all speed, to be my wife.

CROMWELL   At once, Sire.

TEACHER   But Cromwell and Holbein were not being honest. The portrait Holbein painted looked nothing like Anne of Cleves, and they were worried as they escorted Anne to the King, some weeks later. Listen to what happened. Henry is seated in one of the royal rooms when a knock comes at the door. The servant, always with His Majesty, with a nod from him, opened the door to admit Cromwell and Holbein, the artist.

CROMWELL   Your Majesty, we have accompanied Madam Cleves.

HENRY   Bring her in, come on, let me meet my lovely bride.

CROMWELL   Sire, I will. (*As he goes out he whispers to*

	Holbein, waiting outside the room with Ann.) He's going to be livid. I had no idea how unattractive the woman is. What made you paint such a picture?
HOLBEIN	I thought to please him, but I hoped there was someone else, other than this one, for his bride.
CROMWELL	A foolish thought, we might lose our heads for this.
HOLBEIN	Ah, don't say so.
ANNE	(*in a heavy German accent*) Your Majesty. It is wonderful to see you.
TEACHER	As Anne rose from her curtsey, Henry gasped. Quickly recovering himself, he said,
HENRY	Greetings, Madam. Please be seated. I will be with you in a moment. Cromwell, a word with you.
TEACHER	And, bowing to her, he beckoned Cromwell to follow him, meeting Holbein waiting outside.
HENRY	(*seething with anger*) What is the meaning of this? You deceitful imbeciles. How dare you bring this ugly creature to me, pretending that she is the young woman in the painting? Who was that, eh? Some slut you bribed? I warrant you'll be sorry. And now, you escorted her here, you can escort her back.
CROMWELL	But Sire, Your Majesty, you cannot send her back. Your people will never understand. One divorce for a king is one thing but sending a Princess back immediately she arrives, will create huge political upheaval, even war.
HENRY	Escort her to her royal chambers and I will

see her presently, but not as a wife. The very thought of that is abhorrent to me. She's as ugly as sin. Now, get out, both of you.
(*Cromwell and Holbein bowing low, leave backwards.*)

TEACHER But at the insistence of Henry's ministers, Bishop Cranmer married Henry and Anne on January 6th 1540, three days after they met and only eleven days after Jane Seymour's death. Two years later the marriage was dissolved. Nineteen days after, on July 28th 1540, Henry married again, this time to Catherine Howard.

CHILD He must have been a horrid king. Marrying so many people and so near to the death of one.

TEACHER Yes, he was in that way, but he did have some good points. Many people believe he was always fat and ugly but although he might have been when he was old, as a young man he was apparently very good-looking and charming. He enjoyed music and its composition. His best known piece of music is the song 'Greensleeves'. Active in sport, he enjoyed riding and tennis. He was a soldier and also very proud of his navy. One of his ships was the *Mary Rose* and I'm sure you've all heard of her sinking. Here's a little scene about it that you are going to read.

It was in July 1545 that Henry, with some officers and courtiers, followed by many citizens, went down to Portsmouth to watch the *Mary Rose* in the Solent, so here's what happened.

Scene 6

CAST

A NAVAL OFFICER
HENRY VIII
6 COURTIERS
6 CITIZENS

NAVAL OFFICER	Sire, all seems quiet after the battles of yesterday.
KING	Indeed. The French came out in force, I hear.
OFFICER	Yes, Sire. Early this month the French came into the Solent Channel, between Hampshire and the Isle of Wight. More than two thousand ships and thirty thousand men.

KING	Yes, yes and they engaged with our ships, did they not?
OFFICER	They did, but little harm was done to either side, thank God.
KING	But now we are here to see the *Mary Rose* named for my sister and our Royal emblem, the rose. The flagship of my Lord High Admiral, Sir Thomas Howard. Well, where is she?
OFFICER	I am sure she will sail out soon, Sire. It seems, as the evening approaches, a breeze is beginning to get up. But Sire, why don't you rest awhile? Sit here. You will see her immediately she comes out.
KING	Thank you, yes, I will. (*He sits, the officer stands behind him. Courtiers range behind him. Citizens come closer.*)
CITIZEN 1	Oh look, the King is sitting down.
CITIZEN 2	I wonder what is going to happen.
CITIZEN 3	P'raps the *Mary Rose* isn't sailing today.
CITIZEN 4	Don't be silly. Of course she's sailing. That's why the King is here.
CITIZEN 5	Who are you calling silly? (*He raises his fist at Citizen 4.*)
CITIZEN 6	Oi, no fighting. We'll be turned away. I for one want to stay and see the ship.
CITIZEN 2	So do I. I hear she's had a number of refits. Improvements, I expect.
CITIZEN 1	Yes. She's the Lord High Admiral's flagship. She's got to be good.
CITIZEN 3	Wait, His Grace is standing up. Something must be happening. (*They push forward.*)
COURTIER 1	Oh, do stop pushing, you wretched citizens.
COURTIER 2	Yes, you'll have us in the water next.
COURTIER 3	I can't imagine how people like that got here.
COURTIER 4	Nor I. Just go back, scum.

COURTIER 5   Heaven help you if His Majesty hears you.

COURTIER 6   Exactly. Be quiet, all of you.

CITIZENS   (*together*) What's it to do with them? We have every right to be here. We're the King's subjects, same as they are.

KING   At last, she comes. The *Mary Rose*. Ah. What a sight. Magnificent. Look! The French advance. The *Mary Rose* prepares to do battle. The sails unfurl. Look, her men are on deck. What? An upper deck? That's new. Done to take on more crew, I'll wager. Cheer my people. Wave to them, my courtiers and citizens. Give them a cheer. Let's show them how proud we are. (*Everyone cheers.*) But the crew. What are they doing?

OFFICER   They're moving to starboard, Sire.

KING   What? All of them? What for?

OFFICER   They are anxious to see you, Sire.

KING   The fools. Where are the officers? She's listing badly. My God, she's sinking.

CITIZEN 4   He's right. The King is right. The crew has overturned her. Oh my God.
(*Everyone is crying and shouting at once.*)

COURTIER 5   Not only that, the gun ports are open. The water is pouring in.

CITIZEN 2   They were made too low to make it stable. But they should have been closed. Why weren't they?

CITIZEN 5   Someone should have seen to it.

COURTIERS   She was top heavy. Those brass canons. Too heavy for the size of the ship.

CITIZEN 3   It was the upper deck made her top heavy. Too many men up there.

COURTIER 3   It was as she made a turn. The wind took her.

CITIZEN 4   My God, she's gone completely under.

KING   Have none escaped?

OFFICER   Maybe thirty or so, Sire. A handful. Of course, many of them were Spaniards and couldn't understand our language.

KING   Oh God save their souls. A tragedy. The netting, I suppose. Put across the decks to prevent enemy boarding, but it meant the men couldn't escape. (*Sadly, the King turns away. Then the courtiers and citizens go off, shaking heads, clasping hands.*)

TEACHER   That must have been a terrible thing to watch. To see all those men go down with the ship.

CHILD   It made me feel very sad, Miss.

CHILD   Me, too.

TEACHER   Yes, but you know that now she has been lifted from the sea bed and is in a special museum in Portsmouth, don't you? In 1971, a spring tide, combined with a severe gale, uncovered several structural timbers on the sea bed and it became clear that the *Mary Rose* lay on her starboard side. In 1979 the Mary Rose Trust was formed and an archaeological team, under the direction of Dr Margaret Rule, CBE, with Prince Charles, began work to excavate the wreck. On October 11th 1982 the wreck was lifted from the water onto a support cradle and put into a dry dock to be treated. And when they were searching on the sea bed, they discovered not only weapons, tools, crockery, cutlery, coins and musical instruments, but also hundreds of the remains of the poor sailors and soldiers who had drowned.

CHILD   Can we see the *Mary Rose*, Miss?

TEACHER   For those who live near Portsmouth, yes.

CHILD   I'd love to go to Portsmouth. Could you take us, Miss?

TEACHER   We'll have to see. But now, let us find out more of the Tudors. Two years after the sinking of the *Mary Rose*, King Henry died and his son, Edward, became King Edward VII, then aged ten, a staunch Protestant like his father.

               But Edward never regained strength, and there were people who had reason to worry that he would die young and leave the throne to his half-sister, the strongly Catholic Mary. They wanted the country to stay as Henry VIII made it, Church of England, so they started planning. Listen now and you will know what these plans were.

Scene 7

CAST

DUKE OF SUFFOLK
DUKE OF NORTHUMBERLAND, Regent for Edward VI
LORD GUILDFORD DUDLEY, son of Duke of Northumberland
LADY FRANCES BRANDEN

SUFFOLK   Now listen, but not a word outside this room.
NORTHUMBERLAND   Of course not, but what are we to hear?
SUFFOLK   We all know that Edward is a sickly young man, weak from his birth.
GUILDFORD   Yes, but what is your point?
SUFFOLK   My point is this. When Edward dies, which could be soon, who is the next on the throne?
NORTHAMPTON   Mary, of course.
GUILDFORD   Yes, and that means...
SUFFOLK   A Catholic England.

100

NORTHUMBERLAND   And God forbid, after all Henry did to promote the Church of England and Protestantism.

GUILDFORD   So what can we do?

SUFFOLK   I'll tell you my plan. My daughter, Lady Jane Grey, by right of her birth great grand-daughter of Henry VII, has as much right to the throne as Mary.

NORTHUMBERLAND   And Guildford, my son, would make an excellent king by her side.

LADY BRANDEN   But she is only a child.

SUFFOLK   Ten years of age, yes, but she is a good, obedient girl and will do as I say.

GUILDFORD   But the time is not yet.

SUFFOLK   Correct. But I propose to enter her into Court under the protection and tutelage of Katherine Parr. She has no children of her own. I am sure Jane will be most welcome.

NORTHUMBERLAND   And the purpose of this?

SUFFOLK   She will be introduced into the ways of Court life. Katherine is a true follower of Henry VIII, a staunch Protestant, so my daughter Jane will flourish under the true religion. Then, when the time comes, she will be ready to be queen.

GUILDFORD   This is dangerous talk. If we were heard...

SUFFOLK   That is precisely why I cautioned you all at the beginning of our discussion. This must be between us. And Lord Guildford, later I shall give you my daughter's hand in marriage.

GUILDFORD   Marriage? But your lordship...

SUFFOLK   Don't thank me, man. It will be arranged when the time comes. Now, we will go our separate ways. Keep silent.

(They go off separately.)

101

Scene 8

CAST

KATHERINE PARR, widow of Henry VIII and now Mrs Thomas Seymour
LADY JANE GREY

Lady Jane is seated at court with Katherine Parr. They are talking.

KATHERINE Little Jane, such a sweet child, I am delighted that your father has entrusted you into my care. We shall get on well, don't you think?

JANE Yes, I think so. I'm glad too, to be here. But what am I supposed to be doing?

KATHERINE You will of course continue your studies, Latin, Greek and, of course, the arts and your social skills, dancing and holding conversations, and then you will be like a queen.

JANE A queen? You do not mean that, Madam, I will never be a queen.

KATHERINE Would you not like to be?

JANE No, I would not. But you didn't mean that, did you?

KATHERINE Do not worry. I only said 'like' a queen.

JANE I'm glad of that because the very thought of being a queen fills me with horror. Never would I want to be one.

KATHERINE There, child. Do not get so upset. Come, we will walk in the garden for a while. It will ease your spirit. You look quite agitated.

JANE My apologies, Madam. I was shocked by the thought of your calling me a queen.

KATHERINE Come now. Think no more of it. Let us enjoy

the flowers. The roses are particularly fine... (*They go off.*)

TEACHER   Well, let us find out what happened next. First, let me tell you that some years have gone by and Lady Jane Grey was married in May 1553 to Lord Guildford Dudley.

CHILD   Did she get to be a queen?

TEACHER   Yes she did, but wait. The time has now passed several years. Edward has been king for six years, but his health has become worse, and in 1553, he became very ill and died. So now listen.

Scene 9

CAST

NURSE
NORTHUMBERLAND
KATHERINE PARR
PAGE
DOCTOR

NURSE   (*running into the page*) Quick, quick. Get the doctor. Call his Grace the Duke. It's the King. King Edward. He's taken a turn for the worst.

PAGE   Which first?

NURSE   Oh, don't be such a dim wit. The doctor, then the Duke of Northumberland.

PAGE   Right.

NURSE   And hurry!

PAGE   All right. (*He runs off.*)

KATHERINE   (*enters*) What has happened? Oh, is it the King? Oh, Lord help us.

DOCTOR   (*hurrying in*) Nurse. Come with me to His Majesty's room. (*They start to go, then, enter the Duke of Northumberland.*)

NORTHUMBERLAND   Nurse, you sent for me. The King – he is dying you say? Doctor, have you seen him yet?

NURSE   We are just going to the royal bed chamber, your Grace.

NORTHUMBERLAND   Then I shall come with you.
(*They all go off.*)

TEACHER   The King was very ill and he died the next day. It was July 1553. Then, those who had plotted to make Lady Jane queen after Edward's death, realised that they had to move fast so again a meeting was called. Listen.

Scene 10

CAST

NORTHUMBERLAND
DUKE OF SUFFOLK
LORD GUILDFORD DUDLEY
KATHERINE SEYMOUR
LADY JANE GREY

NORTHUMBERLAND   The King is dead. We must announce the succession at the same time. Now is the time to declaim Jane as queen.

SUFFOLK   She has always said she does not want to be queen. But there must be no delay.

GUILDFORD   I believe she will be persuaded. As her husband I shall insist.

NORTHUMBERLAND   Then call in Mrs Seymour and the Lady Jane.

GUILDFORD   I had better do so. What we are to discuss must be for no other ears. (*He goes to the door and calls*) Come, Jane, and you, Mrs Seymour.

(*Lady Jane and Katherine Seymour enter.*)

GUILDFORD   Now, my dear wife, as you know, King Edward is dead and so another must take the throne. Your father, the Duke of Suffolk, the Duke of Northumberland and I are agreed that that shall be you. You have been well tutored in the ways of the court by Mrs Seymour. Is that not true, Madam?

SEYMOUR   It is, my Lord. She has all the learning and attributes of a true queen.

LADY JANE   But I have never wanted to –

GUILDFORD   Enough. This is our decision. We cannot allow the Catholic Mary to come to the throne. You, as the great grand-daughter of Henry VII have every right to be queen and we must remain true to the Church of England. Now we will make haste for everything to be ready for your coronation.

(*They go off. The Duke of Suffolk has his arm across Jane's shoulders.*)

TEACHER   Lady Jane really did not want to be queen, did she? But only four days after Edward's death she became the monarch.

CHILD   What happened next, Miss?

TEACHER   The Duke of Northumberland, learning of Mary's anger (who considered herself to be the rightful heir), gathered a force of soldiers to fight against Mary as she, with her troop of men, rode to

London from Suffolk intending to take the crown from Lady Jane Grey. It was nine days after Jane had been crowned queen that Mary rode in with her troops and had Jane and her father, the Duke of Suffolk, sent to the Tower to be executed. The saddest thing was that even Jane's own father had turned against her before his death, hoping to save his own life by proclaiming Mary Queen of England. Lady Jane and her husband (Lord Guildford) were kept in the Tower but were not executed until after a second ill-fated uprising in her name.

Now, you may remember that Henry was very fond of Mary, but when Edward was born, he sent her away because she was no longer his heir. But after Edward's death and when Lady Jane had been forced to give up the throne, Mary was crowned Queen Mary I of England on October 30th 1553. One of her first actions was to reinstate the marriage of her parents (Henry VIII and Catherine of Aragon) as legal. At the age of thirty-seven she married Philip of Spain in Westminster Cathedral. The people were not pleased. Listen to what they said.

Scene 11

CAST

ANN, a housewife
BETTY, a serving maid from an inn
JOHN, a blacksmith
JOSEPH, a stable hand
CROWD (including speaking parts for LEADER and A MAN)

BETTY	I heard talk in the inn last night.
JOHN	(*laughing*) Oh yes? Listening again, were you?
ANN	Stop teasing, John. Let Betty tell us what she heard.
BETTY	Well, I will. There were some well-dressed men and they were talking about the Queen – saying she's going to mary!
JOSEPH	About time too. She's bound to want an heir.
JOHN	Did they say who she was going to marry?
BETTY	Well, I did hear summat about Spain.
ANNE	Spain? She's going to marry someone from Spain?
JOSEPH	Did you hear a name?
BETTY	Sounded something like Pip.
JOHN	That must be Philip of Spain.
JOSEPH	If she's heard aright, that must mean she's going to marry a foreigner. By'r lady. That's not right. There'll be a riot among the people, you'll see.
JOHN	You're right, my friend. There's plenty of English noblemen for her to choose from. Why take a foreigner?
ANNE	She's supposed to be stubborn, I expect she wouldn't take advice from anyone.
JOSEPH	Well, she should. She ought to think of her people.
BETTY	Wait a minute. Listen. (*They listen and soon they hear a lot of shouting as a group of people come towards them.*)
CROWD	(*shouting angrily*) The Queen Traitor. She's deceived us. A prince from Spain, marriage.
JOSEPH	What did I tell you? They must have heard of the Queen's marriage. I said there'd be a riot. We had better get out of the way.
	(*As they leave, the leader of the crowd calls.*)

107

LEADER	Have you heard? The Queen has betrayed us. She's going to marry a Prince from Spain.
A MAN	She's executed enough of the people. It should happen to her.
LEADER	Come on. Let's get a proper crowd. Down with the Queen!
TEACHER	And so the people showed their feelings and wanted the Queen to know it. But something else nearly happened. Listen.

Scene 12

CAST

SUFFOLK, based in Leicestershire
SIR THOMAS WYATT (THE YOUNGER), from Kent
SIR JAMES CROFT, from Herefordshire
SIR PETER CAREW, MP for Devon

At the home of the Duke of Suffolk

SUFFOLK	(*to Sir Thomas Wyatt*) You requested this meeting? Between the four of us.
WYATT	Yes I did. I am very angry at the way the Queen is behaving, to marry a Spanish Prince, a foreigner. It will put our beloved country at the risk of being mastered by another power. Who knows when it will end. We already know that Mary proposes to bring the Kingdom of England back into the Church of Rome and to restrict the rights of Protestants in the land. Now are we all here Protestants?
ALL	We are.

WYATT	None Catholic?
ALL	None.
WYATT	Suffolk, can we be overheard?
SUFFOLK	Absolutely not. That is why I suggested here in this house. The walls are thick and the doors are locked
WYATT	Then I propose that we muster a force to arrest the Queen and replace her with her half-sister, Elizabeth Tudor, a committed Protestant who, it is planned, would then marry Edward Courtenay.
SUFFOLK	By God, a courageous plan. It will need much working out. But I like this proposal. Bold. I would still wish to claim that my daughter, Lady Jane Grey, is the rightful heir to the throne. But ... your plan has merit.
CAREW	This is fine talk but how do you propose to achieve this? The Queen has many loyal subjects who would not agree to her arrest.
CROFT	It would need a joint effort. So, come on let us have some details.
WYATT	Very well. My plan is that the four of us should arrange an uprising in our own counties, then with our men, ride to London and take over the throne. After that we shall replace Mary with her half-sister, Elizabeth. In the meantime, French ships shall be dispatched to prevent Philip making his way to this country. How say you?
CROFT	Agreed.
CAREW	Agreed.
SUFFOLK	And I.
WYATT	Very well. We will begin our journeys. You, Sir James, will go to your land in Herefordshire to raise an army. You, Sir Peter, to Devon,

and I shall return to Kent. Let us shake hands and wish each other God speed.

TEACHER   And God speed was echoed by all, as they made their way to begin their rebellion.

CHILD   And was it a success, Miss?

TEACHER   No, I'm afraid not. One after another, for different reasons, they dropped out. Thomas Wyatt was the only one who reached the outskirts of London with four thousand men. But even he was stopped by the Queen's soldiers at Ludlow. He was later tried and executed with nine hundred and ten of his men. At his execution Mary I took away his title and his lands. At the same time Lady Jane Grey, her husband and her father were taken from the Tower and beheaded – as punishment for her father, the Duke of Suffolk's part in the Wyatt Rebellion, even though Jane had had nothing to do with it. And then Elizabeth was taken to the Tower, through the Traitor's Gate, even though she was no traitor. Courtenay, the man it had been arranged she was going to marry, was exiled by Mary who had been crowned Queen in October 1553.

CHILD   How long did they keep Elizabeth in the Tower?

TEACHER   For two months, then she was sent to Woodstock Manor, in Oxfordshire but later she was allowed to return to her childhood home in Hertfordshire. Only a few months later, Mary married Philip of Spain and they were called Queen and King. Mary was not a popular monarch, and she is mostly remembered for restoring the Catholic faith in England. When she died, childless, in 1558, Elizabeth became Queen. Unlike Mary,

Elizabeth was well liked. She was intelligent and she spoke several languages; she loved sport, particularly horse riding, hunting and hawking; she was also brave and forthright. As she said in a speech at Tilbury Docks, when she reviewed the troops about to set sail in battle, 'I may have the body of a weak and feeble woman, but I have the heart and stomach of a King, and a King of England too.' She also loved the theatre and particularly enjoyed the plays of William Shakespeare. It is believed that his play *Twelfth Night* was the result of a request from her to write something amusing for the season of Twelfth Night after Christmas.

Elizabeth was the last of the Tudor monarchs. When she came to the throne England was a country torn apart by religious arguments but when she died at Richmond Palace on March 24th 1603, England was one of the most prosperous and powerful countries in the world.

Let us finish their history on a light note. The Tudors were lovers of the theatre and acting. At first, travelling players would set up a stage on a travelling cart; gradually they took their craft and performed in inn yards, with audiences all around. The theatres developed from these inn yards, so that when the first theatres were built they were made in the same shape. Shakespeare called his theatre a wooden 'o', meaning it was circular, but in fact Tudor theatres were more horse-shoe shaped, with a covered gallery above the 'stage'. The wealthy people sat or stood on the gallery, while the poor had to stand on the floor, which had no roof, so if it rained they got wet. They often had a changing room under the gallery and a space under the stage from which a trapdoor could be opened for a special entrance, such as a ghost, or devil. They did have scenery, some of it extremely elaborate, and highly colourful. The battle scenes were always very noisy, with fireworks and crackers let off in the fields around, but there was no room for canons or horses. In fact in the chorus' speech before *Henry V*, Shakespeare wrote, 'Think when we talk of horses, that you see them, printing their proud hoofs i' the receiving earth.' Our modern Globe Theatre has been built on the exact lines of those in the Tudor age, so if you can visit, you will feel that you are taken back to the time of the Tudors.

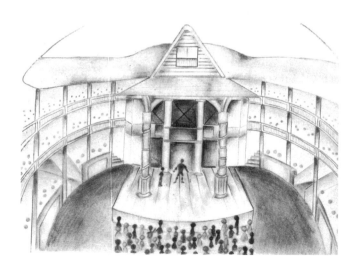

Questions

Scene 1

1. This scene is called 'The views of the people'. What sort of people were they?
   a. Actors   b. Politicians   c. Peasants
   How do you know?
2. What did they hope the new king would be like?

Scene 2

1. What was it that Henry VIII wanted Wolsey to do?
2. What facts did he use to persuade the Pope to agree to his request?

Scene 3

1. When Henry's request to the Pope was refused, what was he determined to do?
2. Why was Henry so anxious to have a son?

Scene 4

1. For how long did Henry wait, after the death of Anne, before he married Jane Seymour? Write a few sentences saying what you think of his behaviour.

Scene 5

1. What did Henry ask Cromwell to do for him?
2. Who was Holbein? What did he do for a living?
3. Why was Henry so horrid to Anne of Cleves?
4. Why did Henry at first believe her to be a great beauty?

5. What song did Henry write? When you have the answer, ask your music teacher to play it for you, and choreograph a dance for ladies and gentlemen at court.

Scene 6

1. Henry VIII was proud of his navy so, accompanied by a naval officer, courtiers and citizens, he went to Portsmouth to see the *Mary Rose* sail out of the harbour to do battle with the French. Imagine you are a reporter for the Royal newspaper and write an article on the reasons for the sinking of the ship.

Scene 7

1. Why did the Duke of Suffolk say his daughter (Lady Jane Grey) was legally in line for the throne?
2. Why did the Duke not want Mary Tudor to be Queen when Edward died?

Scene 8

1. Did Lady Jane Grey want to be Queen? How do you know the answer to this question?

Scene 9

1. Write a poem about the death of Prince Edward.

Scene 10

1. For how long was Lady Jane Grey Queen?

Scene 11

1. When Mary Tudor did, after all, become Queen, who did she marry?

Scene 12

1. What did Thomas Wyatt propose?
2. Was his plan successful?
3. When Mary died, Elizabeth (her half-sister) became Queen. Write an article about Elizabeth, showing her character, her interests and how she helped to make England a great country.
4. Elizabeth loved Shakespeare's plays. Which was the one she asked him to write? Why? And at what season?

Follow-up Work

1. Looking at the illustration, draw a picture of the *Mary Rose*.
2. In a craft lesson, make a model of the Globe Theatre.
3. In groups of three or four, construct a family tree of Henry VIII's wives, daughters and son. You will probably need some help from your teacher for this.

Research Sources

On the Trail of The Tudors, by Richard Wood (Franklin Watts)

Exploring the Tudors by Dr Brian Knapp (Curriculum Visions)

Tudor World (Exploring History) by Haydn Middleton (Heinemann)

THE ANCIENT EGYPTIANS

A play in three scenes with 26 parts

When the children have come into the classroom, the teacher will tell them they are going to learn something about the ancient Egyptians, but that there were so many different civilisations, she cannot concentrate on all of them. The total civilisation of Ancient Egypt lasted nearly 3,000 years, from about 3,100 to 30 BC (before Christ).

The lesson begins with a Greek historian called Herodotus, who visited Egypt in 450 BC and spoke to the people. The children are asked to imagine that they are Egyptian children living at the time.

PROPS required: A drum, drawings for Imhotep to show the Pharaoh.

Scene 1

CAST

HERODOTUS
NARRATOR
SCRIBE 1
SCRIBE 2
FATHER
CHILDREN:
SHABEN (boy)
ASENET (girl)
RHAMADAN (boy)
AMUNET (girl)

NARRATOR	Listen, all you people of Egypt. Herodotus speaks.
	(*a roll of drums*)
HERODOTUS	You should be glad, people, for I tell you, Egypt has a gift. It is the gift of the Nile.
	(*The people murmur and nudge each other.*)
NARRATOR	Silence. Listen.
HERODOTUS	A gift of the Nile. It is true, for without the Nile, you would perish.
SCRIBE	What does he mean?
FATHER	Let him explain.
HERODOTUS	Yes, I will explain. Think of the flooding, that which we call the inundation.
SHABEN	Oh this is boring, we have heard it all before.
ASENET	Well, I haven't, so listen.
SHABEN	Who are you to tell me to listen? You're always talking anyway.
ASENET	Oh no I'm not.
SHABEN	Yes you are. Chatterbox.
ASENET	Oh go and jump in the river.

118

NARRATOR	QUIET.
HERODOTUS	I will finish. When the flood comes, lasting from July to December, it brings down the black fertile silt on the land called Kenet.
FATHER	Indeed, fertile land where we can grow our crops.
HERODOTUS	As you say. And it is called the Black Land.
RHAMADAN	And the land where the flood hasn't been we call Deshret.
AMUNET	Know-all. Clever head.
RHAMADAN	Well I do know. I learned it from my father. He's taught me all this history.
AMUNET	Of course you did. We all learn from our father. He's our teacher. Where else? Magic?
FATHER	And I shall have to teach you children how to be quiet.
SHABEN	Oh, let Herodotus get on with it, do.
HERODOTUS	An annoying group here.
NARRATOR	I agree. Now everyone must be quiet or they will be punished. (*Glares at them and shakes his fist. The children imitate the narrator in mime.*)
HERODOTUS	I wish you farewell. Remember, your gift is the River Nile.
NARRATOR	Now, come forward, scribes. You are the writers, are you not?
SCRIBE 1	We are and we have recorded the history of our land.
SHABEN	What – all of it?
SCRIBE 2	Who is this insect?
SHABEN	Who are you to call me an insect?
NARRATOR	All children are to be quiet
SHABEN	Yes, Sir! (*With a wink to the others.*)
NARRATOR	Tell us please, some of our history.
SCRIBE 2	Well, in some ways we are the same as our

119

ancestors. But we have discovered that 200,000 years ago, our ancestors lived in tribes. They made flint tools, things like hand axes, arrow heads and knives. And they hunted and killed animals.

RHAMADAN (*to Amunet*) How could they do that? Had they already learned about making handles?

SCRIBE 2 If you must interrupt, I suppose I'd better tell you.

SCRIBE 1 I think I am more equipped to do that.

SCRIBE 2 Oh? Why?

SCRIBE 1 I was the scribe who interpreted the wall pictures.

SCRIBE 2 True, but don't make too much out of it, and keep to the facts.

SCRIBE 1 Accusing me of lying now? I think we shall have a discussion after this.

SCRIBE 2 If you mean a fight, I'll tell you now. I'm not the fighting sort.

SCRIBE 1 Oh, really?

NARRATOR Can we please get on?

SCRIBE 2 Certainly, if my fellow scribe will allow it. The fact is, we think our ancestors wielded much of the tools by hand first, although no proof has been found. But certainly later, animal horns were used as handles, with leather strips for joining. As we do now.

SHABEN I can imagine them chasing the animals. (*He and Asenet chase each other.*)

SCRIBE 1 Behave, you children. And when the animals were caught, the women cooked them in clay ovens.

RHAMADAN But what else did they eat? Were there any farmers?

AMUNET Did they have vegetables? Corn?

120

SCRIBE 1   Oh yes, just as we have now. It was the peasants who farmed the land and produced food for the whole community.

SCRIBE 2   Some years the peasants would grow three types of crops. As well as corn, many varieties of vegetables were grown and these were very welcome for they could be eaten raw.

NARRATOR   Of course, as we know even now, there must be enough food for everyone in the land, but also for the gods.

SCRIBE 2   As it is written by our ancestors. It is the gods who must be given food, or the flooding might fail.

SHABEN   And then what?

NARRATOR   We would have no silt, so no Black Land, to sow our crops. And we would starve.

SCRIBE 2   And the Pharaoh would not be able to speak to the gods on the people's behalf.

RHAMADAN   Well, we still work in families, don't we?
AMUNET   Like our ancestors.

NARRATOR   If you didn't you wouldn't survive. No one person could grow enough food. But let us look at something else our ancestors did. They respected the elderly of the tribe. Even the great grandfather would be the chief of them all, until he died.

RHAMADAN   Well, we do still. We haven't got a great grandfather...

SHABEN   But our grandfather is still alive.
ASENET   And we have to do as he says, always.
SCRIBE 1   Yes, it is true that not much has changed in our society for centuries.

SCRIBE 2   A good thing too. Certainly in that children are expected to look after their parents when they are old.

121

ASENET	What did children play with?
AMUNET	Did they have the same sort of toys as we do?
SCRIBE 1	From what we read and discover they had rag dolls, balls, hoops and sticks.
SHABEN	How do we know these things?
SCRIBE 1	A lot of toys have been found in the tombs of children.
RHAMADAN	Can it be proved that they were children?
SCRIBE 1	Yes, mostly, because they have been found with a lock of hair over their face, just as you have, which proves they were children, since that lock of hair is cut when the child becomes adult.
SCRIBE 2	Not forgetting the pictures of them in wall paintings.

Scene 2

CAST

NARRATOR
CHILDREN:
  SHABEN
  ASENET
  RHAMADAN
  AMUNET
THE PHARAOH
HIS DAUGHTER
HER COUSIN, MANESSEH
QUEEN
SCRIBES 1 & 2
PRIEST
A NOBLEMAN

In this scene the scribes, the narrator and the children can be played by others, although they are intended to be the same people as in Scene 1. The nobles and their family are non-speaking and can be played by other children.

NARRATOR   We are now going to learn about the Pharaoh, his Queen and the work of the priests.

SHABEN   I expect they had easy lives.

ASENET   Not having to work like the peasants.

RHAMADAN   Like us, you mean, working to keep alive. (*Pretends to cry*)

AMUNET   Cry baby boy! No wonder women are more important than men.

RHAMADAN   You stupid girl, I was pretending. Anyway, even if we think women are more important, we don't think the same of girls.

ASENET   Well, you should.

NARRATOR   May we get on?

RHAMADAN   Yes, all right (*making a face at Amunet*).

NARRATOR   Good. So, let us imagine that we are in the court of Pharaoh in the year 450 BC. The same year we were in before.

PHARAOH   Listen, my family in the court. We all know that it is my duty to preserve the present dynasty as our great ancestors the Kings did before us. We cannot allow our family to die out, for, unlike our peasants who are kept together by their working tribes, in order to survive, we must maintain our blood line.

QUEEN   How right you are and it is my place, as the matriarch, to see the noble line prospers through me.

PHARAOH   Of course. In a land where the royal line stems through the Queen, it is right that you

123

	should tell our daughter the plans we have for her.
QUEEN	As you say. Now, daughter, come here, together with your first cousin Manesseh. (*They approach the Queen.*) We, the Pharaoh and I, have decided that you, daughter, are ready for marriage, and so that, as we have been saying, we may keep our blood line, you will become the wife of your first cousin. (*The two young people bow and, taking hands, move away.*)
NARRATOR	This arrangement is perfectly normal and works in a similar way with the peasants. As we have heard, the peasant tribe has to work as a unit and so marriages take place between people of the community. A girl can marry any man, of high status or low, and at about the age of eleven her parents will consult with the parents of an older male to arrange the marriage.
SCRIBE 1	As you know, for much of this hasn't changed over the years, there is no word for wedding, and no religious ceremony. The 'bride', followed by friends and family, simply walks from her father's home to that of her husband. She is married, usually for life, though divorce is not unheard of.
ASENET	Tell us about the work of the priests.
NARRATOR	Well, of course, but I think this may be more the work of a scribe, since they have recorded the history. But remember, all you are told about the year 450 BC may well correspond with our priests today.
SHABEN	But tell us.
SCRIBE 1	Very well, I will tell you. Temples were

124

built as huge buildings, constructed in stone and were called 'the fortress of the gods'. No ordinary person was allowed inside, only the priests and the King were let in. Hear what a priest has to say

PRIEST   People, I speak to you as your sacred priest on this day of the Festival of the god Opet. You all may watch the procession from outside the Temple although, as you know, no ordinary person may enter the building. It is my duty to carry the statue of the god Amun-Re into the sacred boat for the first part of the journey.

NOBLEMAN   (*bowing low*) We wait for the wonderful sight of the great Amun-Re. Will you allow the people to ask their favours from the god?

PRIEST   My permission is granted, but the favours may be craved only when we have boarded the sacred boat.

NOBLE   And will the god make the boat tilt as an answer?

PRIEST   Indeed, as usual.

NOBLE   And when the statue of the god is carried on the shoulders of your fellow priests, may the people begin their festivities?

PRIEST   Of course, let the music and the festivities begin.

           (*The people cheer and the music begins.*)

(At this point, if the teacher thinks fit, it could be suggested to the children (as Egyptians) that, at a later time, they could devise some festivities and music for themselves.)

SHABEN   I enjoyed that, but was that all the priests did? Carry the god's statue?

125

NARRATOR	No. Because they were always clever men, and could read and write, they used to spend part of their working life as a scribe.
AMUNET	Seems strange, a priest working part-time.
SCRIBE 2	Yes, but we cannot alter history and that was the way, then.

Scene 3

CAST

NARRATOR
CHILDREN:
  SHABEN
  ASENET
  RHAMADAN
  AMUNET
SCRIBE 1
SCRIBE 2
IMHOTEP
GUARD
PHARAOH

NARRATOR	Now we are going back in time, a long, long way, round about two thousand years in the past.
SHABEN	You've got a good memory. (*The children laugh.*)
NARRATOR	Don't be so cheeky.
SHABEN	Sorry.
NARRATOR	So I should think. I don't know what's come over children these days. When I was young ...
SCRIBE 1	I'm sure your past history must be interesting, but I don't think it tells us of the pyramids.

126

NARRATOR	Of course, you're right. Will you continue?
SCRIBE 1	I will, but it will mean another change of time in our history. So, let us imagine that we are in the time of Imhotep, who is believed to have lived from 2667 to 2648 BC, because we believe he was probably the first man to design a pyramid.
SCRIBE 2	He was a Vizier (a most important official to the Pharaoh Djoser), an astronomer, a priest and a doctor. Listen now as he visits the Pharaoh.
GUARD	Welcome most high Imhotep, master, great Vizior to our Pharaoh. May I announce your arrival to the Great One?
IMHOTEP	Oh, I don't need all that bowing and scraping every time I arrive. Just go and tell him I'm here and I want to see him, immediately.
GUARD	Sorry, I'm sure. May I tell him your business then?
IMHOTEP	No you can't. Just tell him I am here.
ASENET	That told him.
SHABEN	I wouldn't dare.
AMUNET	Well, I would. He sounds pompous. I'd dare to tell him.
RHAMADAN	You're as bad as he is. I think you're bluffing.
AMUNET	No, I'm not. I would dare.
SHABEN	Oh leave her. She always thinks she's better than everyone else.
AMUNET	No, I don't.
SHABEN	Shh. Listen.
GUARD	The Pharaoh will see you now.
IMHOTEP	Of course he will. Move aside.
	(*He rushes past the guard, and arrives to face the Pharaoh.*)

127

PHARAOH	Ah, there you are. You look troubled. What is wrong?
IMHOTEP	It's that bull of a guard of yours. Every time I come, he insists on going through the nonsense of asking my business. Doesn't he know that I am your Grand Vizior, and the most important official at your court and the land?
PHARAOH	He does and he is merely obeying orders. It is strictly forbidden to allow anyone to see me, without having stated his business.
IMHOTEP	Well, I think you might exclude me from all that nonsense.
PHARAOH	Take care, you go too far.
IMHOTEP	Very well, but I have some important news. As an architect I often take time to design buildings and so on.
PHARAOH	Yes. Well?
IMHOTEP	I have some drawings here to show you. But first let me explain. I was working on a design for a tomb for when your highness

should need it and began with a rectangular shape called a mastaba, as usual. Then I drew a wall around it, but realised that it could not be seen from the outside. So I drew a series of smaller mastabas on top of the first, until it was sixty metres high. Thus it would be seen from Memphis, the capital city. So, almost by accident I had designed what I will call a pyramid.

PHARAOH   Indeed, a very worthy idea. Do you imagine it will be repeated?

IMHOTEP   I am sure of it. It has the makings of a splendid tomb, for royalty of course.

PHARAOH   Very well. We will dwell on the idea. You may go now.

IMHOTEP   Farewell, Excellency. I believe I have created a long-standing and useful building. (*He leaves the palace.*)

NARRATOR   And so he had, for after that, the big pyramids that we can see today were eventually built. Now, Imhotep is respected as a god of architecture and of medicine. But after his step pyramid (so called because the sides went up by steps) the three great pyramids were built at Giza. Guarding these pyramids is a huge stone statue called a Sphinx. This creature has a large stone body of a lion and a human head.

AMUNET   Why is the Sphinx there?

NARRATOR   Don't you know? It guards the pyramids which hold the bodies of the Kings, who are the most important people so that even in death they must be in the best place.

RHAMADAN   What did our ancestors think about death?
SCRIBE 1   Perhaps I should answer this.

NARRATOR   Yes, please do.

SCRIBE 1	Well, their beliefs were really the same as ours. As we do, our ancestors believed in the after world; they thought that when a person died he would go through various places, where he would be examined to see if he was fit for the final resting place. *(Children nod and murmur 'yes' and 'of course'.)*
SCRIBE 2	May I continue? *(Scribe 1 nods.)* They thought that once there they would be as they were in life and they would join with family and friends who had gone before.
AMUNET	If they had been good.
SCRIBE 2	Of course.
SCRIBE 1	So this is why they developed the skill of preserving bodies which we know are called 'mummies'.
RHAMADAN	Can you tell us some more about mummies?
SCRIBE	As now, it was of course only Royalty, Kings, Queens and pharaohs, who were mummified and placed in magnificent tombs within the pyramids. With them were placed many wonderful objects, which had been their possessions in life, clothes, furniture, jewellery, even rich food.
SHABEN	What else?
TEACHER	That, I think, will have to do, as we return to the 21st century. You have taken part in a small 'slice' of Egyptian history and there is much information still to find out, some of which we shall do in the class work. But, just to finish, you may have heard of someone called Tutankhamun. He was the youngest Pharaoh and died when he was only nine

years of age. He married and the young couple were moved back to the old royal palace at Thebes. Little is known about him because he died so suddenly and so young. No tomb had been prepared for him, so we don't know whose tomb he occupied. Some of the treasures buried with him had his name carved over another's. He was mummified, but it is thought, hurriedly, because too much resin was added to the bandages, and it leaked downwards and glued Tutankhamun's mummy to the case.

So, that is really enough for now. There are some questions and tasks for you to do, to help you remember all we have done today.

Questions

1. What was the gift that Herodotus told the people about?
2. What tools did the early people use?
3. How was the food cooked?
4. What was the main difference between the peasants and royalty?
5. What was it that Imhotep wanted to show the Pharaoh?
6. Can you think of all the food the peasants grew?

Further Tasks

1. In your craft lesson, make a step pyramid.
2. Draw a picture of the River Nile, showing the black silt on one side.
3. Find, from the internet, a picture of an Egyptian boat, and write a story about the priest putting the god into it and the people asking for things.

4. Ask your music teacher to suggest some suitable music and choreograph an Egyptian (belly) dance.

Research Sources

People Who Made History in Ancient Egypt by Jane Shuter (Hodder Wayland)
Family Life in Ancient Egypt by Peter Clayton (Wayland)
Ancient Egyptian Children by Richard Tames (Heinemann)
Focus on Ancient Egyptians by Anita Ganeri (Franklin Watts)

WORLD WAR 2 – PART ONE

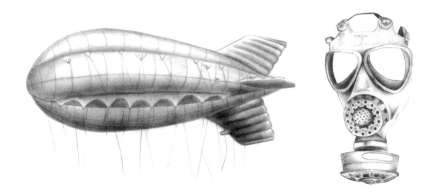

A play in three scenes with 42 speaking parts (if cast separately)

This is a short play to introduce the children to a few of the people who lived during 1939–1945, the years of World War 2.

Props/effects: Table, old-fashioned radio, recording of Neville Chamberlain, recording of air-raid warning and all-clear, DVD of *Goodnight Mr Tom*, recording of doodlebug engine and 'big bang' of a bomb.

CAST

MRS GREEN
MRS JONES
MRS ABBOTT } These ladies are all housewives and
MRS BARNES   mothers with young children at school.
MRS SHARP
MR TURNER, a road sweeper
COLONEL BRADSHAW
CHILDREN:
  BOBBY GREEN
  PENNY ABBOTT
  BERYL JONES
  STEVE ABBOTT
  PETER JONES
  SALLY JONES
  JIMMY JONES
  MAVIS BARNES
  (Other children as non-speaking school children)

Scene 1 The Street

Time: 10.30 am August 10th 1939

The women are standing together voicing their worries about the possibility of war.

MRS GREEN	I don't know how you feel, but I'm very worried.
MRS JONES	About the war, you mean?
MRS ABBOTT	'Course it's about the war. We're all worried sick.
MRS BARNES	But, hang on, it hasn't been declared yet. Mr Chamberlain assured us. 'Peace in our Time' after his visit to Germany. It might be all over before it begins.

MRS GREEN	Yes, and pigs might fly. (*All laugh*)
MRS BARNES	We shouldn't be too down-hearted though. I mean, we really don't know yet, do we?
MRS ABBOTT	No, we don't know for sure, but I bet the government does.
MRS JONES	Why do you say that?
MRS ABBOTT	Well, they're delivering those Anderson shelters to everyone, and we've all to be fitted with gas masks.
MRS GREEN	Ugh, horrid things. We had ours fitted yesterday. We all looked like pigs.
MRS ABBOTT	And the number of air raid sirens. Surely they wouldn't put those up for nothing.
MRS JONES	And the blackout. I had to order yards and yards of blackout material, and then had to make it up to fit all the windows. I hate sewing at the best of times. That was an absolute nightmare.
MRS ABBOTT	I know what you mean. It took me days to finish.
MRS BARNES	And I did hear someone say, the government has made plans to evacuate the children.
MR ABBOTT	Oh don't. That's what I'm dreading.
MRS GREEN	Oh, I don't know … It'd be quite nice to have a bit of peace without always hearing them whining for something.
MRS BARNES	You don't really mean that.
MRS GREEN	Well, p'raps not. But they do seem to take up all my life.
MRS JONES	True, but we wouldn't like to be without them.
MRS ABBOTT	But we may have to be.
	(*They are all silent for a moment, thinking.*)

135

MR TURNER	Morning, ladies. You're looking very serious. Lost a bob and found a tanner*?
MRS ABBOTT	Ha ha. Funny, eh?
MRS JONES	Good morning, Mr Turner. Keeping our road clean then? No we haven't lost a bob and found a tanner. We're talking about the war some of us think is coming. We're worried about our children.
MR TURNER	War? No. Hasn't that clever Mr Chamberlain sorted out old Hitler? He wouldn't dare make war on us now.
MRS GREEN	But the government is preparing for it.
MRS BARNES	We were just saying they've made plans for evacuation of the children.
MRS ABBOTT	And gas masks.
MRS JONES	And air raid shelters.
MR TURNER	Yes, well, they had to do that, to show the Jerries* we wouldn't be taken unawares. See? Well, best get on. Bye all.
WOMEN	Bye, Mr Turner.
MRS GREEN	He's a good soul.
MRS ABBOTT	Yes, but I think he's over cheerful. I mean, apart from all the things we've been talking about, what about the barrage balloons? Surely the government wouldn't go to all that trouble and expense if they didn't think they were necessary?
MRS JONES	That's right. They must cost a lot, too...
MRS BARNES	What are they for anyway?
MRS GREEN	They're to protect us from low flying enemy aircraft.
MRS BARNES	How?

*In 1939 a bob = a shilling (5 pence); tanner = a sixpence (2¹/2 pence); Jerries = Germans.

MRS ABBOTT	From what I understand they're secured to huge concrete blocks on the ground by very strong steel hawsers attached to the lower part of the balloon, so any plane flying beneath would have its wings cut off.
MRS BARNES	Clever, but nasty.
MRS GREEN	Well, war is nasty. Oh look, here comes the Colonel. Good Morning, Colonel Bradshaw.
COLONEL	Good morning, ladies. A very pleasant morning. But I notice that you are all looking a bit down, if you don't mind my saying so.
MRS ABBOTT	We don't mind of course, and yes we are a bit down. We've just been talking about the possibility of war and we're worried.
COLONEL	I'm sure you are and it seems to me to be a very real possibility, dreadful though it seems. That mad Hitler wants to take over the world. Somehow he ought to be stopped and the only way I can see is to fight. It will be hard on everyone, as it was last time, but it may have to be, although I'm sure we all hope for peace.

Sorry, I have to go, I'm supposed to be meeting my wife. Keep smiling, ladies. Goodbye for now. |
ALL	Goodbye, Colonel.
MRS JONES	He didn't help, did he?
MRS GREEN	No, he didn't but he's such a gentleman. I love to see him raise his hat to us.
MRS BARNES	Real old-fashioned, but yes, nice. Well, I must go, too. It's time to get the dinner on. Jack always expects it on the table

when he comes in and the kids will be clamouring for food. Cheerio. (*She goes off.*)

MRS GREEN   Me too. See you later. (*She too leaves.*)

MRS JONES   Yes, better get the spuds on. Bye. (*She leaves.*)

MRS ABBOTT   Off I go. I've enjoyed our chat. (*She leaves also.*)

Scene 2

London railway station. August 31st 1939, very early in the morning. A group of people including the people in scene 1 and their children.

MRS ABBOTT   This is it. I never really thought it would happen, but it has. (*To Penny, her little daughter*) It's all right darling, you'll enjoy going on the train.

PENNY   But where are we going, Mummy?

MRS ABBOTT   (*Looking at Mrs Jones, who is holding her son, Jimmy's hand*) I'm sorry, Penny, I don't know yet. We haven't been told.

MRS GREEN   That's right. (*To Bobby, her son*) Don't sniff, Bobby, use your handkerchief.

BOBBY   But it's the clean one teacher told us to bring.

MRS GREEN   All right. Use this one.

MRS BARNES   It's a crying shame not to tell us where our children are going. As soon as possible they told us but for all we know it could be Timbuctoo.

MRS GREEN   I hardly think so, but I hope they tell us soon.

MRS ABBOTT   But what worries me is the little they have

138

been told to take. Gas mask, handkerchief, toothbrush, comb.

MRS BARNES   And only one change of clothes. Oh, I just hope they'll be all right. (*To her daughter*) You will look after little Jessie, won't you, Marian?

MARIAN   'Course I will, if she doesn't cry all the time.

JESSIE   (*sniffing*) I don't cry all the time, but I wish we didn't have to go away.

MRS GREEN   Poor little thing. That Hitler's got a lot to answer for.

MRS JONES   Yes, but let's try for the children's sake, to look on the bright side.

MRS ABBOTT   You're right, but it seems awful, all these children leaving home for the first time, not knowing where, having no idea who they'll be staying with, or in what kind of home.

MRS BARNES   Well, we're in the same boat. I shan't sleep a wink until I know where mine are. I think Marian will be all right, but it's little Jessie who really worries me. She's so little she, (*whispers to Mrs Abbott*) sometimes wets the bed.

MRS ABBOTT   Yes, I imagine that must be a worry for you, but let's hope there'll be some nice motherly folk to take them in, who've got children of their own.

MRS BARNES   Let's hope so.

MRS GREEN   Here comes the train. Let's hope it'll be less crowded than the Tube. That was dreadful, stifling.

MRS JONES   I heard they closed seventy-two stations on the underground so that all the children could travel at the same time. Stand still,

	Jimmy, you don't want to fall under the train when it gets here.
JIMMY	'Course I don't, but I want to go to the toilet.
MRS JONES	Well, you can't now. There'll be one on the train.
JIMMY	Yes, and I bet everyone will want to go.
MRS JONES	Well, you'll have to wait your turn, won't you? Now, you'll be getting on the train in a moment. Sure you've got everything? Now don't worry, dear. They say we can visit you later, when we know where you are and you've settled in. And I'll write to you as soon as I have your address.
SALLY	Will the people be kind to us, Mum?
MRS JONES	I hope so, love.
MRS ABBOTT	Seventy-two? Good Lord, that must have taken some organising.
BOBBY	Mum, I'm frightened. I don't want to go.
MRS GREEN	Don't be frightened, Bobby. You'll probably like it when you're there. I expect you'll make lots of new friends.
SALLY	Mum, will we go to school there?
MRS JONES	Yes, 'course you will. You've got to keep learning.
SALLY	Yes, I know, but the teachers might be horrid to us.
MRS JONES	Of course they won't, though I expect they'll have a lot of work to do with more pupils in their class. But Peter will look after you, won't you, love?
PETER	If I have to. Yes, I will.
MRS JONES	Good boy. There now. Time to go.
MRS ABBOTT	Come on now. The doors are opening. Time to get into the train. Up you get.

MRS GREEN	Bye bye. Take care. I'm sure you'll enjoy it. (*The children are in the train, with many others. The parents are all waving and calling goodbye. The children wave from the train, as the train puffs its way out of the station.*)
MRS JONES	I feel like a good cry. I can't bear them leaving us.
MRS ABBOTT	I know dear, and I feel the same. But we've got to realise that if the war does come, at least they'll be safe from the air raids.
MRS BARNES	You're right. We've got to be thankful for that.
MRS GREEN	Tell you what, let's go to the station buffet and have a cuppa. Oh, hallo Mrs Sharp, love. Been to see your lads off? I expect you feel as we do – a bit low, so we're going to have a cuppa. Coming with us?
MRS SHARP	You're right about feeling low. Yes. I'm ready for a cuppa. (*They go off to the station café.*)

Scene 3

The Church Hall, Sunday, September 3rd 1939

CAST

MR BARNES
MRS BARNES
MR GREEN
MRS GREEN
THE VICAR, THE REVEREND MORTON
MR ABBOTT
MRS ABBOTT
VILLAGERS

(The hall is filling with villagers. They are asking each other why they have been asked to come to the hall instead of the church since it is Sunday. Among the crowd are the ladies we met in scene 1, with their husbands.)

MR BARNES	This is a rum do. I suppose we are told to be in the hall because there are too many of us to use the church.
MRS BARNES	That's right. But why? And I wonder why that wireless has been put on the table at the front.
MR GREEN	I've got a good idea.
MRS GREEN	Tell me.
MR GREEN	Shh. 'Ere comes the Vicar.
VICAR	Good morning, people. I have asked you to come here instead of the church for the reason I'm sure you have guessed. The church is really not large enough to accommodate us all, and as I understand there is to be an important wireless message from our Prime Minister, Mr Chamberlain, I wanted all of you to be present. (*He turns on the radio. After a few crackles the sound begins.*)

CHAMBERLAIN'S VOICE:

'I am speaking to you from the Cabinet Room at No 10 Downing Street. This morning, the British Ambassador in Berlin handed the German Government a final note, stating that unless we heard from them by 11 o'clock that they were prepared at once to withdraw their troops from Poland, a state of war would exist between us. I have to tell you now, that no such undertaking has been received and that, consequently, this country is at war with Germany.'

MR GREEN	(*After a moment of dead silence*) So, it's happened. After the war to end all wars, 1914 to 1918. With all those lives lost – and Hitler has started another. We thought it couldn't happen again.
MR BARNES	Ah well. It'll be over by Christmas.
MRS JONES	They said that last time, and look what happened.
MR ABBOTT	Well, I shall join up. Back to my old regiment.
MRS ABBOTT	George, you will not.
MR ABBOTT	I'm sorry, Joyce, but I feel I must.
MR BARNES	And I shall join you.
MRS BARNES	No, Jack, no.
VICAR	This is a dreadful state of affairs but I feel obliged to say that the church service must begin. We have to applaud those who wish to serve their country, but now is not the time for hasty decisions. What will happen we must believe is God's will and we must join together in prayer and ask for his guidance. Come along, into the church. (*Some follow the Vicar, but others walk away, some obviously in tears.*)

Questions

When you think that you really understand part one of this play, answer the questions below, in writing.

1. In the beginning, what were the signs that war was coming?
2. What was the main fear of the women talking in the street?
3. What did the road sweeper mean when he said 'Lost a bob and found a tanner'?

4. By looking again at the script, find out how many tube stations were closed on August 31st. Why?
5. Find out all you can (from the library or the internet or ask an older person) about what an Anderson shelter looked like. Draw a picture of one, and then write a description.
6. What did the women do after the train left the station?
7. Why did we go to war with Germany?
8. What was the name of the Prime Minister at the time?

Further Tasks

1. In groups of five, imagine you are evacuees (children being sent away to safety), and make up a little play which tells how you would feel.
2. A friend has asked you to explain a barrage balloon, its use, and what holds it up. Do this in a group of three, one wanting to know, one talking and one drawing the balloon and how it is secured to the ground.

After this, read *Goodnight Mr Tom* by Michelle Magorian or ask your teacher to show the video/DVD of the film. It is an enjoyable story which will help you to understand the early days of the war.

TEACHER   That must be all for today. We will read/act out part two next time.

WORLD WAR 2 – PART TWO – THE BLITZ

To the teacher

Before beginning this part, I would hope that the children have been able to watch the DVD of *Goodnight Mr Tom* because I think they will more readily understand part one and will gain more from that which follows.

Before the children come into the classroom, the room should be in a state of total shambles; desks overturned, papers strewn (as if it had been devastated by an air raid). If possible, a space at the back of the room could be sectioned off to serve as a shelter. Ideally, as the children enter, a recording of the Blitz could be heard. After a few moments this may be turned off and the children called to stand round the teacher's desk.

TEACHER	Now, look at your classroom. Can anyone tell me why it looks like that?
CHILD	There's been an air raid.
TEACHER	Right. Now we're going to enact a little play about that but we will imagine that we are looking at a bombed house. Some of you will take part. Here are the characters you will be.

Scene 4

CAST

AIR RAID WARDEN
POLICEMAN
OLD MAN
LADY HOLDING HER CAT
CHILDREN

POLICEMAN	This is pretty dreadful. A direct hit, I'd say.
WARDEN	You'd say right. What a tragedy.
OLD MAN	I heard it all right. Thought it was coming down right on our shelter. Killed were they?
WARDEN	Yes ... dreadful. Grandparents and two kids. Father in the Forces, mother on night duty at the hospital. They don't know yet.
LADY	How dreadful. When will this horrible bombing end? Every night for the last month. London, Coventry Cathedral ...
POLICEMAN	They nearly got St Paul's last night. Stood for hundreds of years that has and Hitler's blasted murderers nearly wiped it out.
LADY	My poor Sophie was so terrified by the noise, I almost lost her. *(A recording of the air raid siren blares out. All rush to the shelter.)*

146

WARDEN	Come on young 'uns, into the shelter. Careful now. Mind the stairs. Don't fall down.
CHILD 1	My mum said that lots of people go down the Tube station.
CHILD 2	And my mum told me that there are shelters underneath the big shops in London.
CHILD 3	Yes, Swan & Edgar.
CHILD 4	And Selfridges.
POLICEMAN	That's right. They had their basements specially adapted.
CHILD 5	I'd like to see underneath one of those shops.
CHILD 6	So would I.
CHILD 7	Well, I expect I have seen one of them at least.
CHILD 8	How could you have done?
CHILD 7	When my mum used to take me shopping in the West End, we often went down to the basement to buy something. Usually things like kettles, saucepans and things like that.
CHILD 8	Yes, but you haven't seen the shelter.
CHILD 7	I know that, stupid. I didn't say I had.
CHILD 8	Don't call me stupid.
LADY	Now, now children, don't argue. Life's too short for that.
CHILD 7	OK. Sorry. (*Recording of the 'all clear' sounds.*)
OLD MAN	Ah, there's the all clear. Best get home for a cuppa before the next one. Bye all.
ALL	Bye (*They all leave the shelter and come to the teacher's desk.*)
TEACHER	Now, tell me what you thought of that.
CHILD 1	I didn't like it much. The noise of the air raid made me deaf.
CHILD 2	Yes, I felt deaf too.
TEACHER	Well, when it was a real raid, it was dreadfully

147

noisy. Not only the sound of the bombs falling but the guns firing – they were called Ack-ack guns – and the drone of the planes. Then nearly always the sound of the siren on the fire engines.

CHILD 4   I was wishing I was back where I was evacuated. That was so quiet and peaceful. We didn't hear any air raids.

CHILD 5   I liked the place, but I did miss my mum a lot.

TEACHER   I think the government might want you to go back after all these dreadful raids.
(Chorus of yes/no from the children.)

TEACHER   Well, we don't know yet so don't worry about it. Next time we shall look at another period during the war.

Questions

1. What happened at the beginning of part two?
2. The lady with the cat told of past raids. Where were they?
3. Which of the London shops made their basement into a shelter?
4. Why did one of the children say he had been in one?
5. Imagine you have just listened to an air raid; write a poem about your feelings.

WORLD WAR 2 – PART THREE

To the teacher

This part is concerned with doodlebugs and rockets. For this
we return to the people we met in the first part, and some
from the second part, who can be played by the same children
or others. Other characters have been introduced so that more
children can take an active part in the drama.

When the children have settled down, the teacher tells them
that they are going to look at another part of the World
War 2 drama.

Scene 5

CAST

MRS GREEN
MRS JONES⠀⠀⠀⠀These ladies are standing outside the Post
MRS ABBOTT⠀⠀Office, as before, airing their woes about
MRS BARNES⠀⠀the war
AIR RAID WARDEN
POLICEMAN
NURSE
EX WREN (injured and therefore out of the Navy. She walks
with a limp.)
SHOPKEEPER
POST WOMAN (Sandra)
BYSTANDERS (not speaking)

MRS GREEN	Things seem to have quietened down lately.
MRS JONES	Yes. Not so much bombing.
MRS ABBOTT	Well, maybe not, but there's a threat of the Germans sending over some pilotless planes.
MRS BARNES	Pilotless planes? What nonsense. It isn't possible.
MRS ABBOTT	Well, I heard something about it on the wireless. Apparently their engines sound like any plane, though a bit louder, and then when it cuts out, the plane comes down and the bombs it's carrying blow up the target, whatever it is – house, church, school, anything.
MRS BARNES	Can it be true? Do you really believe it?
MRS JONES	I believe I heard something about them when I was in the grocers but I didn't pay much attention. It seemed too far fetched.
SANDRA	(*coming out of the post office*) Morning ladies.
LADIES	(*together*) Morning, Sandra.
SANDRA	You look very serious. Anything wrong? More than usual?
MRS GREEN	Well, yes. Mrs Abbott here has been telling us about these pilotless planes. Have you heard of them?
SANDRA	Doodlebugs? Yes, I've heard of them. One fell on the cricket ground in the next village a few nights ago. No one was hurt but it ruined the cricket pitch.
MRS GREEN	I bet it did. But, what did you call them? Doodle something?
SANDRA	Doodlebugs. I don't know where the name came from, but it seems to have stuck.

150

MRS ABBOTT	Well, I hope they don't come here. They give me the creeps.
MRS BARNES	They'd give you more than that if they fell near here.
MRS JONES	It doesn't bear thinking about. (*The air raid siren sounds.*)
WARDEN	Come on, all of you. Just got a message from HQ, it's one of them doodlebugs.
POLICEMAN	He's right. Look, there it is. Can you see?
MRS BARNES	Yes, I can see it. Oh my god, the engine has cut out. Come on, let's hurry to the shelter.
WARDEN	That's right. At the double. It'll come down near here. Hurry to the shelter. (*They all run to the shelter.*)
MRS JONES	Whew. That was a rush, but I'm jolly glad to be here in the shelter. But I'm that puffed. I'm not used to running.
MRS ABBOTT	Perhaps you should do more, you'd lose a bit of weight.
MRS GREEN	Speak for yourself. But I know I could lose a bit.
MRS ABBOTT	Sorry, I shouldn't have said it though.
MRS GREEN	Oh don't worry. It's true anyway. (*A horrendous bang is heard. They are all silent for a moment, then all speaking at once.*)
ALL	The school! (*The all-clear sounds but without waiting a moment the ladies rush out.*)
MRS JONES	It's OK. The school's OK.
MRS BARNES	Yes, but look at the church. (*They all turn and look.*)
SHOPKEEPER	(*coming out of the shelter*) My shop. Is my shop all right?

151

MRS BARNES	I think it must be. It's just the church, I think.
NURSE	(*coming out of the shelter*) What's happened? Is anyone hurt?
POLICEMAN	Doesn't look like it. But (*to the warden*) I think we'd better go and see.
WARDEN	You're right. Come on then. (*They go off.*)
EX-WREN	(*limping as fast as she can*) Whatever was it? That awful noise, but it suddenly stopped and then there was this terrific bang. I looked out ... I'd been in my Anderson and saw the church on fire.
MRS ABBOTT	The policeman and the air raid warden have gone to see if anyone is hurt and to judge how much damage has been done to the church.
EX-WREN	Oh dear, I do hope the Vicar is all right. I saw him in the vicarage garden not long ago. I know his wife is in the town shopping but, oh dear, the Vicar.
NURSE	Well, we'll soon find out.
EX-WREN	Look, the fire on the church is spreading.
SHOPKEEPER	And here comes the fire engine. That was quick.
EX-WREN	But what did it? I heard a plane as the siren went off and then it seemed to cut off.
MRS JONES	It was one of those doodlebugs.
EX-WREN	A what?
MRS JONES	Doodlebug. A pilotless plane.
SHOPKEEPER	What did you call it?
MRS GREEN	A doodlebug.
EX-WREN	Well, I've never heard of such a thing.
NURSE	Nor have I. But I must get back to the hospital. I'm supposed to be off duty but I must get back in case there are any injured.

152

EX-WREN	I think I'll get back too. I'm not too good yet at walking.
SHOPKEEPER	I'd best get back. There might be some customers waiting. Cheerio.
	(*Chorus of 'cheerios' as every one begins to make their way home.*)

Scene 6

September 1944

The same neighbours are chatting as usual, this time outside the grocer's shop. Suddenly, the shopkeeper rushes out.

SHOPKEEPER	Have you heard?
MRS GREEN	Heard what?
SHOPKEEPER	That Hitler, he's got another weapon.
MRS JONES	What sort of weapon?
SHOPKEEPER	Well, that's just it. Something bombed 'somewhere in Essex', they said on the wireless this morning.
MRS BARNES	Something? Well, it must have been a bomber plane. What else could it be?
SHOPKEEPER	That's just it. No plane was heard, no siren went off. Just a terrible explosion and two of the pubs and a row of cottages, devastated.
MRS ABBOTT	(*joining the group*) What now? You all look scared half to death.
SHOPKEEPER	Hardly surprising. I've just been telling them all about a bombing somewhere in Essex last night.
MRS ABBOTT	Yes? Well, nothing new about that.
MRS BARNES	No, except that it was a terrific bomb but no one heard it coming and there was no siren sounding.

153

MRS ABBOTT	What was it then?
SHOPKEEPER	No one knows yet.
MRS JONES	Another of Mr Hitler's little tricks.
MRS GREEN	It could have been a mine. A friend of mine in Woodford Green in Essex had one caught in a tree at the bottom of her garden. All the people in the street were woken up at four am and told to get out of their houses and stay out for the day, until the wretched thing had been blown up. She said it was dreadful. They were taken away by a friend who had some petrol and they couldn't come back until nearly nightfall, all the time worrying about the safety of their house. It was OK though, luckily.
MRS JONES	That must have been a dreadful experience.
MRS GREEN	It was awful, she said.
POLICEMAN	Good morning, ladies. Chatting away as usual. I don't know how you find the time for all this chatter.
SHOPKEEPER	What cheek. They all came to do a bit of shopping, not that there's a lot to buy with so much food rationed*, but I told them about this new weapon.
POLICEMAN	The rocket? V2? Yes, we've been told about that. It's pretty dreadful, because no one knows when they're coming or where they'll fall. Quite silent they are, until they reach their target and then bang, wallop!

---

*Rationing came in almost at the beginning of the war and everyone was allowed only a few ounces a week of meat, sugar, butter and one or two eggs. Sweets were also rationed and clothes coupons were issued so that it was difficult to buy any clothes that were not essential. In 1940 the government even banned the sale of new cars.

154

MRS JONES	Oh, good heavens, what'll they think of next?
EX-WREN	(*limping in*) You've obviously heard the news? The new weapon?
POLICEMAN	We have. What a devilish thing is war. Just killing innocent people.
MRS BARNES	But Mr Churchill is always confident. I remember his speeches soon after the war began, 1940 I think it was, when he talked about blood, toil, tears and sweat, that we would have to endure, but victory would come.
MRS ABBOTT	Yes, and after the bombing he toured the country, talking to people. And making speeches on the wireless. He was marvellous.
MRS GREEN	And after Pearl Harbor was bombed in 1941, and America came into the war, Churchill felt confident of an Allied victory.
POLICEMAN	He was an old man of seventy at that time and yet he worked so hard, touring between capital cities and conferences. In fact it was in 1940 that Churchill was elected as Prime Minister and Minister for Defence. He held supreme command in the nation's war effort.
MRS GREEN	My father used to say Churchill was a war monger.
WARDEN	(*coming up to them*) A lot of people would have agreed with your father, but I believe that was because he warned the government before the war that Germany was rearming and possessed far more fighter planes than we did. But he was not believed. They thought he was advocating war. (*Sound of air raid siren*) Hey up, there goes the siren

again. Come on, everybody. To the shelter, quickly.
(*Everyone rushes once again to the shelter, as the scene ends.*)

Questions

1. What did the people call the 'pilotless plane'?
2. How did it differ from an ordinary plane?
3. What was the V2?
4. What positions did Winston Churchill hold in the government?
5. Why did some people call him a war monger?
6. What was the major result of the bombing of Pearl Harbor?

Follow-up Work

1. In groups of four or five, imagine you have been wakened at 4 am by an air raid warden and told that a mine was lodged in a tree at the bottom of your garden. Discuss what you would do during the day, and then act out a scene to demonstrate the activity.
2. Imagine you are a journalist for a newspaper and write a report on either
   a) The approach of a pilotless plane, or
   b) Winston Churchill's visit to a bomb site.

Research Sources

Stories and reminiscences from people who lived through the Second World War are excellent primary source material. Children could be asked to talk to grandparents about what they remember from that time.

JOSEPH AND THE COAT OF MANY COLOURS

A short play in eleven scenes with 26 speaking parts and other non-speaking roles

When the children have come into the classroom and settled down, the teacher tells them that they are going to act the real story of the musical, *Joseph and the Technicolour Dreamcoat*.

If possible, a poster of a part of Egypt could be shown to the children. Also, again if possible, another poster of a scene from the musical.

PROPS: A loose garment for Jacob, a coat of many colours, shepherd's crooks and cloaks for the brothers, a toy knife for the killing of the goat, cloaks for the merchants, and bundles for the travellers and brothers. Food on a tray for the butler to bring to Potiphar would be a good touch, and the silver cup Potiphar has put in the sack of one of the brothers.

Scene 1 Jacob's house

CAST

JACOB
JUDAH
JOSEPH

JACOB	(*speaking to himself*) Why is it that my sons are always quarrelling? And always getting at poor Joseph, the one who is more dear to me, because he is gentle and seemingly very clever, with his amazing interpreting of dreams.
JUDAH	(*entering*) Are you speaking to yourself again, Father? Need I ask what about? I don't think so. It will be about your beloved Joseph, I know. Thinking of that expensive coat you gave him which makes him more objectionable than ever because it makes him feel superior.
JACOB	There you go again, being rude about your brother. I can tell what you're thinking by the tone of your voice. Yes, he is my beloved son and I did give him an expensive coat. But you are all loved and you could have had coats as well if you were kinder to Joseph.
JUDAH	Well, we would be, if he wasn't so boastful.

	All his dreams seem to suggest that he believes himself to be better than the rest of us. It makes us angry.
JACOB	Perhaps if you tried to be nicer to him he wouldn't think that.
JUDAH	Oh, you don't understand. There's no reasoning with you. You think he's perfect. Anyway, I'm going with my brothers to take the sheep to pasture. I'll see you some time later.
JACOB	Is Joseph going with you?
JUDAH	No, I'm pleased to say.
JACOB	Well, take care of the sheep. Farewell. (*Judah leaves him. Jacob waits a moment then calls.*) Joseph. Joseph. Are you there? Will you come here please?
JOSEPH	(*entering*) Yes, Father, you called me?
JACOB	Yes I did, I want you to follow Judah and go down with him and your brothers as they take the sheep to pasture.
JOSEPH	Of course, Father. I will first change my shoes and get my beautiful coat of many colours you so kindly gave me. It is such a splendid garment.
JACOB	I'm so glad you like it, Joseph. Now go as soon as you are ready and take care.
JOSEPH	I will. Farewell, Father.
JACOB	Farewell, Joseph. (*Joseph leaves as Jacob goes out of the room.*)

Scene 2 *The pasture*

PROPS: Coat of many colours, whip for merchants, chair for wife, stool for Joseph, bags for corn, silver cup.

CAST

THE BROTHERS
JOSEPH
REUBEN
MERCHANTS
JUDAH

BROTHER 1	Here comes Joseph. Judah, why did you bring him? He'll only drive us mad with his dreams.
JUDAH	I didn't bring him. Father must have sent him.
BROTHER 2	I suggest we kill him. Let's throw him down this well, and we can pretend to father that a wild beast got him.
BROTHER 3	Good idea. We'll be well rid of him. Look at him swaggering along in that coat. We'll have that off him straight away before we throw him over the edge of the well.
REUBEN	No, I think it better if we lower him into the well and leave him to die.
BROTHER 5	What? And have someone rescue him? No fear.
REUBEN	I hadn't thought of that. (*To himself*) I had and I thought I might be able to rescue him later. But now I can't.
JOSEPH	(*walking up to them*) Greetings, my brothers. Father sent me to you.
BROTHER 2	Oh did he? Well, he didn't know how we would welcome you, did he? Come on, brothers. Let's do it. (*They grab him.*)
JOSEPH	What are you doing? Leave me alone. Don't. You'll tear my coat. *(There is a struggle as the brothers drag off his coat and push him into the well off stage.)*

160

REUBEN   We need some sort of proof if we are going to convince Father that Joseph was killed by a wild beast. I shall take one of the wild goats on the hillside, kill it and use its blood to smear on Joseph's coat. Then Father will believe us.

JUDAH   Yes, that's what we must do to make sure Father thinks he's dead. But look, there are some merchants coming this way. That has given me an idea. If we leave Joseph in the well to die we shall not profit by his death. What if we sold him as a slave to the next lot of merchants who come this way? Then, not only will we be rid of him, we shall make money as well.

BROTHER 4   Well said, Judah. We shall do it. Look, more merchants are coming. Come on, brothers, let's drag him out.

BROTHERS   Right. Come on. Let's get him. (*They drag Joseph out of the well and make him stand on the edge.*)

BROTHER 3   Merchants! Travellers! What say you of this fine specimen of manhood? Make a good slave, don't you think? Forty shillings and he's yours. Look at the strength of him as he moves in my grasp. (*Under his breath*) Be still Joseph.

MERCHANT 1   Fine specimen? Who are you deceiving? You'll not get forty shillings from me.

MERCHANT 2   Wait, I think we could make a profit in the capital. I say twenty shillings. Will that suit? It's that or naught.

BROTHER 5   I say yes, let it be done. Here, I'll throw him to you. But money first.

MERCHANT 2   You had better be truthful. We don't want a

161

	weakling. Right, twenty shillings it is. (*He gives the money to Brother 5.*) Come on then, you. (*He takes Joseph roughly and drags him off.*)
JOSEPH	But ... why? Help me. You're my brothers. Help me one of you. What have I ever done to you?
MERCHANT 1	Quiet, you weakling. Any more from you and you'll feel my whip.
MERCHANT 2	And you'll be gagged. Come on. (*He drags Joseph along.*)
MERCHANT 1	We did well there. I think we'll make quite a bit of money when we take him to the slave market. (*He laughs.*)
MERCHANT 2	You're right, my friend. Come on, we should be there before nightfall. (*They move away.*)

Scene 3 Back at Jacob's home

CAST

JACOB
JUDAH
REUBEN
BROTHERS

JACOB	At last, my boys, you are home, But where is Joseph? And what have you there? His coat. What has happened to it? To Joseph? What have you done?
REUBEN	Father, sit down, we have some terrible news –
JUDAH	(*interrupts*) Joseph, our dear brother, is dead.
BROTHER 2	Killed, by a wild animal...
BROTHER 3	His beautiful coat ripped from his back.

162

JACOB	A wild animal? Oh, my poor Joseph. My boy, so kind, so gentle. Can I believe this? Did any of you have a hand in his death?
BROTHER 5	Father. How can you say such a thing? We are as hurt as you.
JACOB	Give me his coat. Let me see. Ahh, blood. It is true. Could you not have saved him?
BROTHER 4	How we wished we could have done.
JUDAH	It was so sudden. It came from nowhere.
REUBEN	So fast. He didn't stand a chance.
JACOB	Oh, oh. I am heartbroken. Leave me. I must weep alone.
	(*The brothers leave.*)

Scene 4 Egypt, at Pharaoh's court

CAST

MERCHANTS
JOSEPH
POTIPHAR, the captain of the Guard at Pharoah's court

MERCHANT 1	(*dragging Joseph in*) Come on, wretch.
MERCHANT 2	Look happy. We can't sell a miserable shepherd.
MERCHANT 3	That's right. Stand up straight. Here comes Potiphar.
MERCHANT 1	Now bow to him. (*Joseph does so and so do the merchants.*)
POTIPHAR	What's this miserable specimen?
MERCHANT 2	Not miserable, Sir. Just fearful in your presence.
POTIPHAR	As he should be. But what is he to do with me?
MERCHANT 3	He would make an excellent slave, Sir.

MERCHANT 1	He is strong and willing.
POTIPHAR	Hm. What do you want for him?
MERCHANT 2	To you, Sir, a very low price. Fifty shillings.
POTIPHAR	Ha. Take him away. I'm not paying that.
MERCHANT 3	But, Sir, we have brought him a long way to you.
MERCHANT 1	It has cost us that to feed him.
POTIPHAR	Nonsense. I'll give you thirty shillings.
MERCHANT 2	Forty is the lowest we can take. Would you leave us as beggars?
POTIPHAR	Thirty-five and that is my final offer.
MERCHANT 3	Ah, Sir, you make a hard bargain.
POTIPHAR	Take it or leave it.
MERCHANT 1	Very well. We will take thirty-five shillings. Go to him, Joseph.
MERCHANT 2	May he treat you well. Farewell. (*The merchants leave, trying not to laugh.*)
POTIPHAR	What do they call you, wretched cur?
JOSEPH	My name is Joseph, son of Jacob.
POTIPHAR	Hm. Well you seem all right. You will be my slave. Get outside and you will find your companions working in the yard.
JOSEPH	Sir. (*Joseph leaves the room.*) (*Potiphar stares after him for a moment, then also leaves.*)

Scene 5 Some months later

CAST

POTIPHAR
HIS WIFE
HER FRIEND
JOSEPH

164

JOSEPH	(*to Potiphar*) You sent for me, Excellency?
POTIPHAR	I did. I want you to know how pleased I have become with the work you do for me. I feel I can trust you with my house and my lands. I am therefore making you my overseer, in charge of these.
JOSEPH.	Oh, Excellency. I am so grateful, Sir.
POTIPHAR	Then go now and do not fail me. I charge you to guard my property with your life should the need arise. (*He leaves the room.*)
JOSEPH	Excellency, with all my heart. (*He bows and starts to leave but is faced with Potiphar's wife and her friend, who have entered the room.*)
WIFE	I see you have persuaded my husband of your ability.
JOSEPH	But, Madam, I do assure you...
WIFE	Your assurances mean nothing to me. Get away from me. I find your ways impossible. You have crawled your way into my husband's confidence like the horrid insect you are. I warn you, pride comes before a fall, and if I have anything to do with it, your fall will come. Now, go.
JOSEPH	Your wish is my command, Madam. (*He bows and leaves the room.*)
WIFE	(*to her friend*) Detestable man. Thinks he is above us. Did you not notice the arrogance of his bearing?
FRIEND	Indeed I did. Now your husband has given him charge of his house and lands, his pride will make him even more impossible.
WIFE	You are right. Oh, to be rid of the wretched man.
FRIEND	Well, I've had an idea. Wait a few weeks

and then find a way of accusing him of assaulting you. Make it a believable act and with tears and trembling tell your husband. Potiphar won't stand for any servant harming his wife.

WIFE — Brilliant idea. I'll do it. Come, let us work out a plan. (*They leave the room.*)

Scene 6 *Potiphar's private room*

CAST

POTIPHAR
HIS WIFE
JOSEPH
GUARD

Potiphar's wife is sitting on a chair, weeping. Potiphar enters.

POTIPHAR — My dear wife. Whatever is the matter? Why this weeping?

WIFE — (*sobbing*) I hardly dare tell you, husband.

POTIPHAR — Come along. You must tell me. I can't bear to see you like this. Who has hurt you?

WIFE — It was your favourite, Joseph. He, he attacked me.

POTIPHAR — (*angrily*) He did what?

WIFE — Attacked me, he tried, tried, oh, it was dreadful . . .

POTIPHAR — How dare he? He'll be sorry for, this. GUARD!

GUARD — (*enters hurriedly*) Excellency?

POTIPHAR — Get Joseph here. At once.

GUARD — At once, Sir. (*He leaves quickly.*)

POTIPHAR — He'll be imprisoned for this. I thought I could trust him. I was wrong. (*He walks up and*

	down the room angrily.) To attack my wife. The evil man. Perhaps I should order his death. (*Wife smiles, making sure he hasn't seen her.*)
JOSEPH	(*entering with the guard*) You called me, Potiphar?
POTIPHAR	Don't you call me by my name, you, you wretch.
JOSEPH	But –
POTIPHAR	But nothing. My wife tells me of your evil deed.
JOSEPH	My evil deed? I don't understand.
POTIPHAR	A liar as well as a woman beater. You'll pay for this.
JOSEPH	But I –
POTIPHAR.	Enough. Guard, take him to the cells.
GUARD	(*grabbing Joseph*) Come on, you. (*He pushes him from the room.*)
POTIPHAR	(*to his wife*) There, my dear. He'll trouble you no more. Come, let us walk in the gardens. It will bring you peace. (*They go out.*)

Scene 7 The prison

CAST

JOSEPH
BUTLER
BAKER
GUARD

Joseph sits on a stool, whittling a piece of wood. After a moment the butler comes to him.

167

BUTLER	Are you able to translate the meaning of dreams?
JOSEPH	God can show us what dreams mean. Tell me your dream.
BAKER	I too had a dream.
JOSEPH	Tell me.
BUTLER	I dreamed of three bunches of grapes. I squeezed the juice into a cup and gave it to the Pharaoh. What can it mean, Joseph?
JOSEPH	That is a good dream and it means that in three days' time you will be free to return to work. Please do not forget to ask the Pharaoh to release me.
BAKER	And my dream, Joseph?
JOSEPH	Tell me your dream.
BAKER	I dreamed that I was carrying three baskets full of bread and pastries on my head and the birds flew down and pecked on them. What can it mean?
JOSEPH	Oh dear. I'm afraid that is bad news. In three days, Pharaoh will kill you.
BAKER	No, no. You must be wrong. You told us that God would show us what dreams meant, but you were telling me, not God. He would not be so cruel. (*He runs out crying 'No, no'.*)
JOSEPH	(*to the butler*) Poor man. He will die at Pharaoh's command. It is God's law.
BUTLER	As you say, poor man. But I trust you have interpreted my dream correctly also. I long to be out of this prison.
GUARD	(*opens the door*) Baker. Come with me. You are to die in three days. Butler, you are free to go. Hurry, both of you. (*They go with the guard. The baker calling to Joseph.*)

168

| BAKER | You did this. You arranged it. |
| GUARD | Come on, cur. (*They go off.*) |

Scene 8 Pharaoh's court

Two years later Joseph is still in prison, the butler forgot to ask Potiphar for his release.

CAST

PHARAOH
SLAVE
MINISTER
JOSEPH
BUTLER

PHARAOH	(*to his minister*) I am sorely troubled. I have had the most distressing dream.
MINISTER	Can you tell me, Sir?
PHARAOH	Yes. It was so strange. In a field by the Nile, I saw two herds of cows, seven in each. The first seven were very fat, but the second seven were very thin. What can it mean?
MINISTER	I cannot tell. Perhaps we could ask another?
PHARAOH	Yes. Find someone. Ah (*the butler enters, carrying a tray of refreshments*), butler. I do not suppose you could help, but I have been so troubled by my dreams that I am prepared to ask anyone.
BUTLER	Excuse my humble suggestion, your Excellency, but I remember when I was in the prison there was a man called Joseph who could interpret dreams. Perhaps if he is still there, you could summon him.
PHARAOH	Joseph. Yes. Summon him immediately. Slave, go to the prison and get him at once.

169

SLAVE	At once, Excellency. (*He rushes out and after a few moments comes back with Joseph.*)
PHARAOH	Joseph, I have been told of your ability to interpret dreams.
JOSEPH	God can show us what dreams mean.
PHARAOH	I'm sure that's true but what can you do? Can you explain my dreams for me?
JOSEPH	With God's help, I will. Your slave gave me an idea of your dreams as he rushed me from the prison. If I understand correctly you have dreamed of fat and thin cows.
PHARAOH	Yes. Seven fat and seven thin. What can that mean?
JOSEPH	(*after a moment*) I believe this is its meaning. It foretells seven years of plentiful corn and seven years of poor corn. The message is that corn should be saved in the good years to cater for the bad years.
PHARAOH	Joseph, I can see that you are a man of God, so from now you will be my chief minister and as a mark of your exalted office I shall give you your own gold ring and gold chain. You will be almost as important as I am. Now leave me and go about your business, Chief Minister. (*Joseph bows and leaves. After a moment, Pharaoh follows, his slave at his heels.*)

Scene 9 Jacob's house

CAST

JACOB
ALL OF HIS SONS

REUBEN	Yes, Father, you sent for us? What can we do for you?
JACOB	It isn't what you can do, but how we can all manage. You must realise that we are in dire straits. Our corn supply is dangerously low, our cattle are near starvation and we ourselves may soon run out of food.
JUDAS	So, have you worked out a plan, Father?
JACOB	I have. I am determined that you all, except Benjamin, shall travel to Egypt where corn is plentiful and for sale.
BROTHER 4	Why not Benjamin?
JACOB	He is too young for such a journey. He will remain with me. So, the rest of you, prepare what you may need for the journey and leave as soon as you can. Farewell and be wary of robbers on the way.
BROTHERS	We will, Father. Farewell.
JACOB	Farewell, my sons. Return safely.

Scene 9 *Joseph's ministerial room*

CAST

JOSEPH
HIS SERVANT
HIS BROTHERS

SERVANT	Sir, there are men at the door, asking for entrance and wishing an audience with you.
JOSEPH	Do I know them?
SERVANT	No, Sir.
JOSEPH	Have they told you what it is they want?
SERVANT	They say they have come to buy corn.
JOSEPH	Have they? Well, send them in.

171

SERVANT   I will, Sir. (*He goes to the door.*) You may come in. (*The brothers enter.*)

JOSEPH   (*to himself*) Oh God, you have sent me my brothers. (*To them*) You wanted to see me? Why?

REUBEN   Oh, Sir, we have come from Canaan where there is very little corn. We have come to beg for some as we understand you have some for sale.

JOSEPH   (*to himself*) I will test them. Servant, throw these poor wretches into prison.

JUDAH   But prison! Why? What have we done but ask for corn? We have money to pay for it!

SERVANT   Come on. You heard what my master said. To the prison. (*He takes them off.*)

Three days later.

JOSEPH   Servant, bring those prisoners to me. They should have cooled their ardour by now.
(*The servant goes and after a moment brings back Joseph's brothers.*)

JOSEPH   Now, I am sending you home but come straight back and this time you are to bring your youngest brother. I insist. But you, Judah, are to stay here while the rest go. Now the rest wait outside until I give you leave to go. (*They go off. Joseph calls his servant again.*) Servant, get a few helpers and fill the bags belonging to the men I have just sent away with corn.

SERVANT   I will, Sir. (*He goes off.*)

172

Scene 10 Jacob's house

CAST

THE BROTHERS
JACOB

JACOB	You have returned without Judah. Where is he?
REUBEN	We were told to leave him behind.
BROTHER 6	But we must return, and this time Benjamin has to be with us.
JACOB	No. I forbid it. Benjamin will not go.
BROTHER 4	But, Father, the man, obviously of high position, insisted. He said we must.
JACOB	But what if harm befalls another of my sons? Joseph, now Judah and then Benjamin?
BROTHER 3	No harm will come to him. We shall take great care of him.
JACOB	Guard him with your lives then. I shall not rest until his return. And yours of course. Go now. Take Benjamin before I change my mind.
REUBEN	Farewell, Father. Do not worry. We shall return, with Benjamin and more corn.
JACOB	Farewell, my sons. Be safe.
	(*They go as Jacob waves them off.*)

Scene 11 Joseph's ministerial room

CAST

THE BROTHERS
JOSEPH
SERVANTS
GUARD

173

SERVANT   Sir, the men have returned, and with the younger one as you ordered.

JOSEPH   Ah, good. Send them in.

SERVANT   Come in. Remember you are in the presence of the important one, Joseph.

JOSEPH   Is your father well?

BROTHERS   (*bowing low*) He is, oh mighty one.

JOSEPH   Servants, bring food for my guests. Take them into the next room. Give the larger share to the younger one. Then bring me their bags that I may observe the food you will fill them with.

             (*As Joseph watches the servants fill the bags with food, he slips a silver cup into Benjamin's bag before his brothers return.*)

JOSEPH   I hope you are well fed. Then farewell all.

BROTHERS   Farewell, mighty one and thank you. (*They exit.*)

JOSEPH   Guards.

GUARDS   (*entering*) Sir?

JOSEPH   Go after those men and search their bags. They have taken a silver cup. Find it and bring them back.

GUARDS   We will, Sir.

             (*While he waits, Joseph walks up and down impatiently. The brothers return and throw themselves at Joseph's feet.*)

JOSEPH   Which is the man in whose bag my silver cup was found?

BENJAMIN   The cup was in my bag, Sir.

JOSEPH   Very well. You must stay and be my servant. The rest can go home.

JUDAH   Ah, Sir, oh mighty one, let me stay instead of my brother. My father's heart would be broken if his youngest son failed to return.

174

JOSEPH   (*to the servants and guards*) Leave the room. (*When they have gone he bursts into tears as he speaks.*) I am your brother, Joseph. It was God's plan that I was sent into Egypt so that I would be in a position to look after you in difficult times. There are still five more years of famine. You must return home and tell your father that the family must come here and live with me. At last I shall be reunited with my father and all my family. You will leave Canaan and live in Egypt, in Gosben, the very best part. Come, my brothers, let us hug one another, in love and forgiveness.

Questions

1. Which of the brothers did Jacob love best? Why?
2. What did the brothers do to Joseph?
3. Why did the travelling merchants take Joseph? What did they pay for him?
4. Where did they take him?
5. Write a short piece on the Pharaoh's dream.
6. Write Joseph's explanation of the dream.

Follow-up Work

1. Draw a picture, either of the merchants taking Joseph, or of Joseph in the Pharaoh's palace.
2. Ask your music teacher to suggest some music and choreograph a dance suitable for the women in Pharaoh's court.
3. Find the position of Egypt on a globe.

THE CHRISTMAS STORY

This play is in ten scenes. Obviously it will be up to the teacher to decide whether to take a scene at a time, or the whole play at one lesson. Either way, in writing the story as a play, my hopes are that it will prove interesting to the children and help them to understand the drama of Christmas.

Questions and tasks are included at the end of the play and as usual they are only suggestions to be used or discarded as you think fit.

A play with 24 speaking characters and as many as available non-speaking

Scene 1

CAST

ANGEL GABRIEL
MARY
ELIZABETH

Mary, a young Jewish girl, is alone in her parents' house in Nazareth. Suddenly she hears a voice calling her name.

GABRIEL	Mary, Mary, Listen to me.
MARY	Who calls me? What do you want with me?
GABRIEL	I am a messenger from God and I have been sent to tell you that you are to have a son and you will call him Emanuel.
MARY	How can this be? I am but a girl and not married.
GABRIEL	It is the will of God. This child will be His son.
MARY	But –
GABRIEL	No, Mary. No 'buts'. This will come to pass. Farewell.
	(The angel goes, leaving Mary bewildered. In a few days' time she decides to visit her cousin Elizabeth, who is six months pregnant.)

At Elizabeth's house

ELIZABETH	Greetings to you, Mary. Please, sit down. You also are expecting a baby? I have a wait now of only three months but you, a longer wait.

178

MARY	That is true. And that is why I have come to see you. I am so bewildered. After the angel told me that I was to have a child who would be the son of God, Joseph became so strange and said he would put me away, because he did not want me to disgrace my family for having a baby outside marriage, but then he said an angel visited him also and told him it would be right for us to marry and so we did. I just don't understand.
ELIZABETH	Don't worry so much, Mary. God is with you and you should just accept that you, above all women, have been chosen for this truly wonderful event.
MARY	I'm sure you are right, dear Elizabeth, and I will try not to be too worried. But I just wish I could understand. Why me? What have I done to deserve this honour?
ELIZABETH	The ways of God are not for us to question. You must believe in Him and honour His will.
MARY	How wise you are, cousin. I will now return home and wait with patience for the birth of God's son. Farewell.
ELIZABETH	Shalom, Mary. May God go with you.
MARY	I am the servant of the Lord. I shall do as He bids me. For now, shalom, Elizabeth.

Scene 2 The Golden Room of Caesar Augustus, Ruler of Rome

CAST

CAESAR AUGUSTUS
SLAVE
MINISTER

CAESAR	Slave, come here.
SLAVE	Sir?
CAESAR	Fetch my Chief Minister. At once.
SLAVE	(*bowing*) Yes, Sir. (*He goes off. After a moment he comes back with the Minister.*)
MINISTER	You need me, my Emperor?
CAESAR	Yes. Go slave. (*The slave exits.*) Now, I have to tell you that our finances are in a bad way. We must have more money to pay our armies in case of war. So I have decided to make sure that the people are all paying their taxes.
MINISTER	How will that be done?
CAESAR	Listen and I will tell you my plan. We shall levy a further tax on every man and wife. In that way our coffers will be filled.
MINISTER	An excellent plan, Sir, but how may it be carried out?
CAESAR	I shall send my horsemen, and slaves as runners, to tell everyone in the land.
MINISTER	But how will they know where to go to pay this tax?
CAESAR	A good question and I have already thought of the answer to it.
MINISTER	Of course, I had no doubt you would.
CAESAR	Be quiet now and listen. I have decided that everyone will return to his place of birth to register for the payment of this tax. That way there will be no mistakes.
MINISTER	Excellent. But how will the people know how much to pay?
CAESAR	I shall say it is the same for each and everyone. They will be told how much to pay for each person. The bigger the family, the more they must pay. Is that not fair?
MINISTER	Indeed. Is this to begin immediately?

180

CAESAR	It is. Notices must go out to my horsemen and to the slaves. I rely on you to organise a route for each company of horsemen and each group of slaves so that the whole of the land is covered. There must be a responsible minister in each area to oversee the registration, record it and see that it is brought safely to me.
MINISTER	I see you have thought this through in detail, as I would expect from such a brilliant mind.
CAESAR	So you say. Now go. Begin the organisation.
MINISTER	I will, Sir. (*He bows himself out.*)
CAESAR	Flatterer. What a fawning fool he is. But never mind. If he does well, he will be rewarded, if not his head will roll. (*Walks out of the room, looking pleased with himself.*)

PROPS: Broom, blanket, bag of straw, toy lamb, scroll for the wise men, warm shawl for Mary, gifts.

Scene 3 Mary's parents' home in Nazareth

CAST

MARY
JOSEPH

Mary is seen sweeping the floor of the little house. After a moment Joseph comes in very flustered.

| JOSEPH | Mary, I've just met some friends of ours and they told me – Oh dear, I've hurried home to tell you so fast I'm out of breath. I shall have to sit down. |
| MARY | To tell me what? Oh Joseph, you've gone quite |

	red in the face with all that hurrying. Whatever is the matter? What did our friends tell you?
JOSEPH	They told me that Caesar Augustus has issued a decree that we are all to register to pay a further tax, everyone the same.
MARY	Register? All of us?
JOSEPH	Yes, but that's not all. Each and everyone has to be registered in the town of his birth.
MARY	Oh? But –
JOSEPH	No buts, Mary, my dear. It means that we must travel to the town of Bethlehem, because it is the town of David my ancestor and my place of birth.
MARY	But Joseph, Bethlehem. That must be more than a day's journey. How can I go when our baby is due any day?
JOSEPH	I fear it is a journey of many days, not just one, and I realise how hard it will be for you but, apparently it is an order; and we must go.
MARY	Then I suppose we must make ready for the journey. I pray to God that our baby will be safe.
JOSEPH	God will take care of him and us. Didn't the Angel Gabriel himself tell you of our child's birth and that he was to be God's own son?
MARY	Yes he did.
JOSEPH	Well then. How could God let him, or us, his earthly parents, come to harm?
MARY	No, of course not. You are right, Joseph.
JOSEPH	Then come, my dear wife. Gather together our small wants for the journey, some bread, cheese and some wine. Some warm clothes, too and a blanket for our babe, if he should be born on the journey. I'll get our faithful donkey

182

ready for you to ride. A sack of hay for his food he can carry and it will be a soft seat for you on his back. I'll bring his blanket also. Now let us hurry. We must leave before nightfall. (*Joseph leaves the room as Mary begins to gather food and clothing for their journey. After a few moments, Joseph re-enters.*)

JOSEPH Now come, Mary. The donkey is ready and waiting outside. Let me take the basket and then you will be able to mount him.

MARY I'm ready, Joseph.

JOSEPH Then let us go, to Bethlehem.

MARY To Bethlehem. Such a very long way. (*They exit.*)

Scene 4 The journey to Bethlehem

CAST

MARY
JOSEPH
JOSHUA
RUTH
REUBEN
LEAH
JACOB
REBECCA

MARY I am so tired, Joseph. Can we not rest for a while?

JOSEPH Soon we will rest, Mary. We will go on a little further. Our journey is nearly at an end and so far you have done so well. Our faithful donkey has carried you with care. Now look,

	we have good company for here are some of our friends. Shalom, Joshua, Ruth.
JOSHUA	Shalom, Joseph and Mary. This has been a hard journey but apparently one we have to endure.
RUTH	Poor Mary. This must be even harder for you in your condition. When is the baby due?
MARY	Any day now, Ruth. I am fearful that he will be born on the journey.
RUTH	Be brave, dear Mary. There are friends here to help you if that should happen. Look, here come Reuben and Leah. Shalom to you both.
REUBEN	Shalom Ruth, Joshua, Mary and Joseph. What a journey this is! Isn't it typical of our rulers? Order us to do something with no thought of the people concerned.
JOSEPH	I'm afraid you're right, Joshua. I most certainly would not have expected Mary to make such a journey at this time, but for orders from the top.
MARY	I am tired but don't worry too much, my friends. I'm sure I will be all right.
RUTH	Look. Here are Jacob and Rebecca catching up with us. Shalom, Jacob, Rebecca.
JACOB	Shalom all.
REBECCA	Have you noticed the crowds in front of us? I cannot imagine how we will all find lodgings when we reach Bethlehem. There must be hundreds of people making the journey to be registered.
JACOB	It's interesting to learn that we all have the same birthplace.
REUBEN	It certainly is. But for this journey we would never have known. But I can't help thinking that it would have been easier for us all to have registered where we are living now.

LEAH	Have you ever known things being made easier for us?
RUTH	No, I can't say I have.
JOSEPH	Look, the crowds seem to be slowing down. We must be nearing the town. Our journey is almost at an end. Thanks be to God.
MARY	Amen to that, Joseph. The crowds are moving again.
LEAH	I'm ready to drop.
JACOB	Come on, I think we should try to hurry on, or we will find no place to stay.
MARY	You all go on, I am going to stop for a few minutes to stretch my aching back. We'll see you there.
JOSEPH	Yes, go on the rest of you. We shall follow soon. And God go with you.
JOSHUA	Well, if you are sure.
JOSEPH	Yes, go on.
JOSHUA	Then we will and may God be with you.
REBECCA	Take care, Mary.
MARY	I will. We will come soon.

Scene 5 Arrival at Bethlehem

CAST

MARY
JOSEPH
GUARD
INNKEEPER
INNKEEPER'S WIFE
INNKEEPER'S DAUGHTER

MARY	Joseph, just look at that mass of people. What are they doing?

JOSEPH	They seem to be arguing. No. There's a guard, directing them. He seems very angry.
MARY	Oh, Joseph, I'm feeling so tired. My back is hurting.
JOSEPH	Have patience, my dear. Look, there are Jacob and Leah. I can just see them going into a building. Do you see? Up that short rise?
MARY	Yes, I see them. But now the guard is waving people away. Oh dear, I think he is saying that there is no more room to stay. Joseph. What shall we do?
JOSEPH	Do not despair, Mary. I can see the sign of an inn. Let us see if we can find the innkeeper. Come along donkey old fellow. You'll soon be resting as we will. (*They have reached the inn and the innkeeper is standing talking to the guard.*)
GUARD	And that's all. You people, there are no more rooms to be had. (*To the innkeeper*) What a crowd. We just can't find rooms for them all.
INNKEEPER	I don't think our Emperor thought very clearly about how his scheme would work out.
GUARD	You're right, my friend. It's always the way. Those at the top get the bright ideas and we are left to work them out.
JOSEPH	Innkeeper. Excuse me, but we need a room for the night. As you can see, my good wife is very near her time and she must have shelter.
INNKEEPER	Can't you hear? The guard has said there are no more rooms to be had. Go away, and take that donkey with you. Come back in the morning and join the crowd for the registration.
JOSEPH	But what about the inn? A small space is all we need.

INNKEEPER	Go away, I said. You have been told. There is no room at the inn. (*He turns away.*)
MARY	Joseph, what are we to do?
	(*The innkeeper's wife and daughter come out.*)
WIFE	(*whispering to Mary*) I heard what was said and I feel so sorry for you. You look as if your baby will be born at any minute. My husband is right, there are no rooms, but we have a stable at the back you are welcome to use. There are animals in it, of course, but it is warm and dry. If you would like it, my daughter will put in some fresh straw for you.
MARY	Oh, thank you, thank you. I am so tired that a stable with fresh straw sounds wonderful. Doesn't it, Joseph?
JOSEPH	It does. Thank you, good wife. You are very kind.
WIFE	(*to her daughter*) Go quickly and prepare the straw for these two people and their donkey. He'll be at home with the other animals.
	(*She returns to the inn as her daughter runs off, followed by Mary and Joseph.*)

Scene 6 Out on the hillside above Bethlehem

CAST

SHEPHERDS 1, 2 & 3
ANGEL GABRIEL

SHEPHERD 1	The night is clear, my friends, but cold. See how our sheep are moving to be near the hedge away from the wind.
SHEPHERD 2	They're not as silly as some folk would

187

	think. They know how to look after themselves.
SHEPHERD 3	Aye, but would they could stand up for themselves against the dangers of wolves around. Then we could have a little peace from these nights of worry about them.
SHEPHERD 1	Ha! That would be a fine thing. But hardly likely.
SHEPHERD 2	No. It's up to us to keep them safe.
SHEPHERD 3	They are, after all, our livelihood.
SHEPHERD 1	What? What's that light?
SHEPHERD 2	A fearful sight.
SHEPHERD 3	Help! I am blinded.
GABRIEL	Be still, good men.
SHEPHERD 1	What? Who spoke?
SHEPHERD 2	Not I.
SHEPHERD 3	Nor I.
GABRIEL	I spoke to you.
SHEPHERD 1	Who are you?
SHEPHERD 2	Take away the light.
SHEPHERD 3	We can't see you, whoever you are.
GABRIEL	Be not afraid. I am the Angel Gabriel and I have brought to you such wonderful news. No, don't cover your faces. Look up and listen.
SHEPHERDS	(*together*) Wonderful news? What is it?
GABRIEL	Listen. This very night a Saviour has been born.
SHEPHERD 1	A Saviour? Who?
SHEPHERD 2	Where?
SHEPHERD 3	Be quiet. Let the Angel tell us.
GABRIEL	He has been born in a stable in the town of Bethlehem and you are to leave your sheep and go down to see him, where he lies in a manger watched by Mary, his

188

mother, and Joseph, her husband. Go now. Your sheep will be safe. Farewell.

SHEPHERD 1   Bethlehem? A stable?

SHEPHERD 2   A Saviour? Lying in a manger?

SHEPHERD 3   How can that be? Did we dream?

SHEPHERD 1   About the angel, do you mean?

SHEPHERD 2   No. We all saw the angel. Come on, I say we must go. He said our sheep would be safe.

SHEPHERD 3   Yes. I agree. Let us go to see this Saviour. To Bethlehem!

SHEPHERDS   (*together*) To Bethlehem.

Scene 7 *The stable behind the inn*

CAST

JOSEPH
MARY
SHEPHERDS 1, 2 & 3

JOSEPH   Rest now, Mary. Our baby is asleep.

MARY   I will. How sweet he looks. Do you think he is warm enough?

JOSEPH   I'm sure he is. Look how comfortably he lies.

MARY   The warm breath of the animals will help.

JOSEPH   Yes. How they look down at him. As if they know of the importance of his birth.

MARY   Perhaps they do. (*Mary sleeps as Joseph keeps watch. Suddenly there is a commotion outside the stable. Joseph goes to see what it is. The shepherds rush in.*)

SHEPHERD 1   The angel told us.

SHEPHERD 2   A Saviour had been born.

189

SHEPHERD 3	And he's lying in a manger.
JOSEPH	Come in, good shepherds. The angel was right. Here he is next to his mother. He is asleep. Don't wake him.
	(*The shepherds kneel down. They are over-whelmed and do not know what to say at first.*)
SHEPHERD 1	Ah. Look at his tiny hands.
SHEPHERD 2	His little face.
SHEPHERD 3	A Saviour. How can it be?
JOSEPH	He is a gift from God.
SHEPHERD 1	Well, yes, all babies are a gift from God. But ...
SHEPHERD 2	But the angel said we would find a Saviour.
SHEPHERD 3	He told us to leave our sheep, that they would be safe.
SHEPHERD 3	How can a baby be a Saviour?
JOSEPH	The mystery is God's. He will reveal the answer when the time comes.
MARY	(*waking*) Good shepherds, shalom.
SHEPHERDS	Shalom, young mother.
SHEPHERD 1	Did we disturb your rest?
MARY	No, I woke to see my new born baby.
SHEPHERD 2	We came at the angel's bidding.
SHEPHERD 3	He said our sheep would be safe while we were away.
MARY	Of course the angel will care for them in your absence. Do not fear.
SHEPHERD 1	We should have brought a present for the baby.
SHEPHERD 2	But what could we have brought?
SHEPHERD 3	Only a lamb. But we didn't think of it.
MARY	Please don't worry, your presence is a gift, for you came as soon as the angel told you of his birth.

SHEPHERD 1	That's right. We just had to come.
SHEPHERD 2	But now I think we should return to our sheep.
SHEPHERD 3	Yes, we should. Shalom, our little Saviour and your parents. May God always be with you. (*The shepherds exit.*)

Scene 8 The Wise Men

A long way eastwards of Jerusalem, there lived three wise men who studied the stars. Today we would call them astronomers.

CAST

WISE MEN 1, 2 & 3
GUARD
KING HEROD

WISE MAN 1	Brothers, come quickly. I have seen a new star. A marvellous light comes from it.
WISE MAN 2	Yes, I see it. Look, brother.
WISE MAN 3	What a wonderful thing. Never have I seen such a bright star. It must be very special.
WISE MAN 1	So special, I believe it to be an important sign. Let us follow this star.
WISE MAN 2	We will.
WISE MAN 3	We must begin our journey at once and find out where it will lead us.
WISE MAN 1	We will. Let us make ready now. There are instruments we must take.
WISE MAN 2	Yes, and perhaps some warm clothes.
WISE MAN 3	Yes. But come, let us begin and follow this magnificent star. (*They quickly gather some*

	warm shawls, their books and leave their house.)
WISE MAN 1	(*as they are travelling*) You know, brothers, I believe the star is one to tell of the birth of a very important man.
WISE MAN 2	That thought has come to me also. Even more important, I believe it tells of the birth of a king!
WISE MAN 3	A king of the Jews?
WISE MAN 1	But how shall we find such a person?
WISE MAN 2	There is only one person who might know the answer. King Herod himself.
WISE MAN 3	Yes, I suppose so, but how do we gain access to King Herod?
WISE MAN 1	Simply by visiting his palace and politely requesting an audience with him. How can he refuse when we tell him our mission?
WISE MAN 2	Very well, we will. We have travelled so far, we have arrived in Jerusalem, his palace cannot be far away.
	(*So in a short time the Wise Men are walking up to King Herod's Palace. They meet a guard at the main door.*)
GUARD	Halt. Who are you? And what is your business with his Highness King Herod?
WISE MAN 1	We are astronomers from far east of this city. We have been following a star which foretells the birth of a baby who has been born to be King of the Jews. We wish to know where he is, so that we can worship him.
GUARD	King of the Jews? Ha ha. You've got it all wrong. This is the Palace of Herod who IS the King of the Jews!
WISE MAN 2	But we must speak to him. Please tell him we are here.

GUARD	I'll tell him, but I think you'll be thrown out on your ears. Herod can get very angry when he is crossed.
WISE MAN 3	I'm sure he will be interested in what we have to say.
GUARD	I think you're wrong, but I'll go and inform the King. Wait here.

King Herod's Throne Room

HEROD	Guard. What do you want? It had better be important.
GUARD	(*bowing*) Your grace, there are three Wise Men to see you. They crave an audience.
HEROD	Oh do they? What about?
GUARD	They speak of a star which they have followed. They say it tells of the birth of a new King of the Jews.
HEROD	WHAT?! Get out. How dare you speak of another King of the Jews? I am he. I am the King of the Jews. How can there be another?
GUARD	I don't know, Your Grace.
HEROD	Then find out, fool. No. Wait, I will approach my courtiers. They will know. (*He exits in a rage.*)
GUARD	(*goes back to the Wise Men*) He's thrown a fit. He's so angry about the thought of a new king. He's gone to his courtiers; he says they will know.
WISE MAN 1	Well, let's hope he will find out where this new king is. We must give him our gifts.
WISE MAN 2	I think I can understand why King Herod is angry. He wouldn't want another king, would he?

WISE MAN 3	No, but I fear he is going to have to accept it. Shh. Here he comes.
HEROD	Greetings, good astronomers. I am interested in your mission. Tell me at what time did you first see this star, which I hear is very beautiful and which you have been following? My courtiers tell me that God's prophet wrote of the birth of a Saviour in the town of Bethlehem in Judea. If you can tell me when you saw the star, I can work out the age of the child. And I too can worship him.
WISE MAN 1	Your Grace, I have written here an account of our journey from the time we first set out, when we saw the star for the first time.
HEROD	Ah. Excellent. Give me the scroll. Now go on your way to Bethlehem to find this baby, then return to tell me of your experience. Then it will be my turn to visit the baby and worship him. Farewell.
WISE MEN	Farewell, Your Grace.
WISE MAN 2	What a kindly man. His response was as one would expect from one so high born.
WISE MAN 3	I'm not so sure. I know he sounded well enough, but it was the look in his eyes I didn't like. There was evil there.
WISE MAN 1	What nonsense. You always were too imaginative. Evil indeed.
WISE MAN 2	Never mind now. Look, the star is still. It has come to rest in Bethlehem.
WISE MAN 3	It has stopped over a house ... no, an inn. Oh, let us hurry this last part of our journey.

Scene 9 *Inside the inn*

CAST

MARY
JOSEPH
INNKEEPER
WISE MEN 1, 2 & 3
ANGEL

MARY	Oh, Joseph, I am so glad that the innkeeper let us stay in the inn. The stable was all right at first, but I was afraid our baby was feeling the cold. Here we have warmth and food.
JOSEPH	Yes, we are so fortunate. But we can't stay here too long. We do not want to overstay our welcome.
MARY	No, of course not. (*There is a knock on the door.*) Come in.
INNKEEPER	There are three very grand men to see you.
JOSEPH	Grand men? I wonder who they can be. Let them enter please, good innkeeper. (*The Wise Men enter.*)
WISE MEN	We have come to see the new king, to worship Him and bring him gifts.
WISE MAN 1	I bring him gold as befits a king.
WISE MAN 2	I bring him frankincense.
WISE MAN 3	And I, myrrh. See, brothers, here is the baby we have come to worship. So small and, yet, a king. Can it be possible? Our journey was long but so very worthwhile. Let us bow low as we give our gifts.
MARY	Thank you, Wise Men. How wonderful of you to have travelled so far to worship this wonderful infant.

JOSEPH	We are very grateful.
WISE MAN 1	The star led us to you and the babe.
WISE MAN 2	His birth was foretold by the prophet Isaiah.
WISE MAN 3	And we pray for him. But now we must leave and return to Herod, who expressed the wish to be told where he could find this young king and worship him. Shalom, Mary and Joseph and the Heavenly child.
MARY	Shalom, good Wise Men. We wish you a safe return.
	(*The Wise Men move to one side.*)
ANGEL	Wise Men.
WISE MAN 1	Yes? Who spoke? Did either of you, my brothers?
WISE MEN 2 & 3	No.
ANGEL	Listen. I am an angel of God. I am sent to warn you. You must not return to Herod. He has no wish to worship the baby. His purpose is evil for he has planned to kill him and all the children in Jerusalem under two years of age. You must keep away and return by another way. (*The angel leaves.*)
WISE MAN 1	How wicked is Herod? After pretending to worship the baby, he plots to kill him.
WISE MAN 3	You scorned me when I said the look in his eyes was evil – said I was too imaginative.
WISE MAN 2	Yes, well, you were right. So let us make our way. We must avoid Jerusalem at all costs. (*The Wise Men set off.*)

Scene 10 The inn

CAST

MARY
JOSEPH
INNKEEPER
HIS DAUGHTER
ANGEL

MARY	What kind men. To travel such a long way to give our son gifts.
JOSEPH	Yes, Mary. But now we must begin to make our way home. I will call the innkeeper, his wife and daughter to bid them farewell and our thanks. (*He goes off and a moment later returns with the innkeeper and his family.*)
INNKEEPER	So this is farewell.
MARY	It is, but we want to thank you for allowing us to stay in your inn. We have been so comfortable. It is hard to leave.
WIFE	We have enjoyed your company, and the little baby has been so good.
DAUGHTER	We were pleased that we could offer you shelter, first in the stable and now in the house. We shall be sorry to see you go.
JOSEPH	As we are to leave. But shalom, good friends. The time has come for our return to Nazareth.
INNKEEPER	May God go with you. (*Mary and Joseph take their baby and leave. But as they do...*)
ANGEL	Mary, Joseph, this is a message from God. Do not return to your home. Herod will be looking for the child, in order to kill him.

197

	You must flee to Egypt, at once. Stay there until I tell you to leave.
JOSEPH	That is a warning we must obey. Come, Mary, to Egypt.
	(*Mary and Joseph leave for Egypt and there they stay until God's messenger speaks again to them.*)
ANGEL	Herod is dead. It is now safe for your return to Galilee.
	(*And so they came back to their home in Nazareth, where Jesus grew up until he came to manhood. As a boy, he learned the skills of Joseph, who was a carpenter.*)

Questions

1. What did the Angel Gabriel tell Mary was going to happen?
2. Who was it that Mary went to visit? Why?
3. Why did Mary and Joseph and the other people go to Bethlehem?
4. When they arrived at Bethlehem what was the problem they faced?
5. Who was it who helped them to rest in the stable?
6. What did the angel tell the shepherds?
7. Why did the Wise Men travel to Bethlehem?
8. What did Herod say to the Wise Men but what did he really intend to do?
9. Where did the angel tell Mary and Joseph to go?
10. Where was Jesus born and where did he live until he was a man?

Follow-up Work

1. In your own words write the story of the journey to Bethlehem.
2. Find a map of the Ancient East on the internet and see if you can trace the journey from Nazareth to Bethlehem. How many miles did they travel?
3. Draw a picture of the shepherds on the hillside with their sheep.
4. With a partner try to have a conversation about what it must have been like in those days to get from one place to another (no planes, buses or trains, not even bicycles).
5. One of the Wise Men told Herod he had written about their journey following the star. Write what you think he wrote, in diary form.
6. Ask your music teacher to find some music which might fit, and choreograph a dance which could suit young people of Bethlehem in the time of Jesus' birth.

The poet John Betjeman wrote a poem which he called, simply, *Christmas*. You may like to ask your teacher to read it to you.

THIRD TIME LUCKY

When the children have come into the classroom and have settled down, the teacher tells them that for this lesson they are going to read and then act a short play, which is a modern version of a parable in the New Testament, called The Good Samaritan.

This is a story about a man who fell in the street and was ignored by his own people but was saved by someone who was considered inferior. This play follows the plot of the Biblical story but with contemporary characters.

PROPS needed for this play: mobile phone, bicycle, scrap of paper and pen.

CAST

MR GREEN, an elderly gentleman
MRS GREEN, his wife
MR FAWCETT, a businessman
MRS JANE WILLIAMS, a housewife
OLD TOM, a tramp

MRS GREEN	Now, Charles, don't be long or you'll be late for your dental appointment and that would never do. Better take your mobile, in case you want to call me.
MR GREEN	Right, I'll do that, and don't fuss. I've got plenty of time for my appointment. I'll be home well before lunch.

MRS GREEN	Yes, of course, but do be careful. There's a rumour that the old tramp is back. Mrs Cooper next door said she heard he'd been annoying people, begging and then turning nasty. So avoid him if you see him.
MR GREEN	Don't listen to such gossip. I'm sure he's a harmless old man.
MRS GREEN	You're too easily taken in. Anyway, he can't be nice to be near, unwashed, never done a day's work and he sleeps in doorways.
MR GREEN	Poor old Tom. I believe that's his name. You've all misjudged him, I'm sure.
MRS GREEN	Maybe. But go on, get to your appointment. Bye bye.
MR GREEN	Bye. See you.
	(*Mr Green walks smartly down the road as his wife waves and shuts the door.*)
MR GREEN	(*talking to himself*) I wish she wouldn't fuss so. And that Mrs Cooper, never got a good word to say about anyone. Poor old Tom, don't suppose I'll see him anyway. (*He hurries along then suddenly trips and falls.*) Oh dear, I don't think I can get up. I seem to have twisted my ankle. Oh. Help. I wonder if anyone will help me. Help!
MR FAWCETT	(*coming up to Mr Green*) Oh, I say. What are you doing down there? Bit early in the morning for a drink, isn't it?
MR GREEN	But I'm not. I haven't. Oh, will you help me? I've twisted my ankle.
MR FAWCETT	Sorry, old chap. Can't stop. Got a meeting to attend. Someone will help you, I expect. Bye.
MR GREEN	Oh, what can I do? I really can't get up. Oh, if only someone would help me...

202

MRS WILLIAMS	(*stopping beside Mr Green*) Oh dear, what a sight. Can't you get up? Have you tried?
MR GREEN	No, I can't get up and I have tried. Will you help me?
MRS WILLIAMS	'Fraid not. Got to get to the supermarket and meeting a friend for coffee after. I bet someone will come. 'Bye.
MR GREEN	Horrid woman. Why won't anyone help? I really can't get up, my ankle is far too painful. And I must have fallen on my mobile. I can't find it. Heavens, here comes old Tom. Wonder what he'll say.
TOM	Well. Wot's 'ere? Can't yer get up?
MR GREEN	No. Can you help me?
TOM	'Elp yer? Course I can. Wait a tic till I lean me bike against the wall 'ere. Right. Nah put your arm rahnd me neck. That's right. Nah 'old tight and I'll pull yer up.
MR GREEN	Ah, thank you. Oh, that hurts. I can't put any weight on my ankle.
TOM	OK, I'll 'old yer. Can yer sit on me bike? (*Tom helps him onto the bike seat.*) Nah, orf we go. I'll take yer to the 'orspital. Yer'll get that ankle seen ter. Will anyone 'ave ter know where yer are?
MR GREEN	Yes, my wife. I was on my way to the dentist.
TOM	Right, give me the phone numbers and I'll ring 'em.
MR GREEN	How good you are. How can I thank you?
TOM	Yer don't 'ave ter thank me. I just wanted ter 'elp. 'Ere we are. The A & E. Good fing they 'aven't closed it, eh? Nah, I'll go and make those phone calls. Gimme the numbers,

203

then I'll be on me way. Good luck ter yer and God bless.

(*Mr Green writes the numbers on a scrap of paper which he gives to Tom before he cycles away.*)

MR GREEN   (*calls out*) Thank you, Tom, and God bless you too.

Depending on circumstances, this could be used in either an RE lesson or English (e.g. a discussion on language use) or Social Studies, or maybe at an assembly.

Questions

1. What did you think of the reaction of Mr Fawcett and Mrs Williams?
2. Were you surprised to find that poor old Tom, a tramp, would be the only one to help?
3. Which person would you like to be in that situation?
4. Did you find Tom's use of English strange? Why do you think he spoke like that?
5. Could you write a story about someone you could call a good Samaritan?

ANOTHER LIFE OR THE ONE WHO WENT AWAY

PROPS needed for this play: objects for table laying.

CAST

MR BARNES, wealthy businessman
MRS BARNES, his wife
JONATHAN, his elder son
PETER, his younger son

The scene is the Barnes' living room, late evening.

MRS BARNES	Jonathan, your father has been telling me how well you are getting on in the business. He is very proud of the way you have grasped the work of the department. Are you enjoying the work?
JONATHAN	Yes, I am, though I must admit I didn't expect to.
MR BARNES	I remember that you were reluctant at first. But the rest of the staff have told me how willing you are to learn.
JONATHAN	Well, I have to say they're a nice crowd. Good fun to be with and very helpful.
MRS BARNES	Well, Peter, we seem to have left you out for the moment. Now you've left school you will be going into the business.

PETER	Sorry, Mum, but that's where you're wrong. I'm not going into the business. It's the last thing I want to do.
MR BARNES	Peter. What's this? Of course you do. You both have always known you'd make the business your career, as I have. It will be the proudest day of my life when I can have Barnes & Sons on the firm's stationery.
PETER	Sorry, Dad, but you'll have to make do with Barnes & one Son. I'm just not cut out for a business career.
MRS BARNES	But what are you going to do?
PETER	I don't know yet, but I'd quite like to farm.
MR BARNES	Not many farms in London, lad.
PETER	No, but I've decided to move west. Devon, I think.
MR BARNES	Jonathan, did you know about these harebrained schemes of your brother?
JONATHAN	No, I didn't, though I guessed some time ago that he wasn't keen on an office job.
MRS BARNES	But Peter, have you thought this through? Where will you live? What about money? Until you find a job, you're going to be very short of cash.
PETER	Don't worry, I've got a bit saved up from the work I did in the holidays.
MR BARNES	Peter, I'd like you to rethink and come into the firm.
PETER	No, Dad, I've made up my mind. Tomorrow I'm off for another life.
MR BARNES	Tomorrow? That's rather sudden isn't it? Can't it wait until we've talked it over?
PETER	Dad, there's nothing to talk over. I've told you what I'm going to do and nothing you can say or do will change my mind. I'm

	sorry, Mum, but that's it. I'm off to bed now. I've already packed all I need and I want to make an early start. I'll text you when I know where I'm living. 'Night all. (*Peter leaves the room.*)
JONATHAN	Well, there you have it. You'll have to make do with me, Dad.
MR BARNES	Yes, but it's not 'make do'. You're an asset to the company, but I wish Peter hadn't got such weird ideas.
MRS BARNES	(*tearfully*) Just so long as he's safe and happy I can accept it.
JONATHAN	Come on, Mum. It's not the end of the world and he'll be back, I bet.
MRS BARNES	Let's hope so. Anyway, I'm off to bed too. Goodnight. (*She leaves the room.*)
MR BARNES AND JONATHAN	Goodnight.
MR BARNES	I think I'll turn in too. You going to bed yet?
JONATHAN	No, there's a film on TV. I'll watch that.
MR BARNES	Well, goodnight then.
JONATHAN	'Night, Dad.
	(*Jonathan turns on the TV and settles down.*)

Scene 2 *Two years later*

CAST

PETER
MR TURNER, a farmer

MR TURNER	And so you see, Peter, since the foot and mouth outbreak and now this blue tongue thing, I can only offer you half-time work.

207

	It'll mean a drop in your wages but it's that or nothing. I'm afraid I can't afford to restock yet and there are only a few heifers left. Not a lot for you to do. You do see my position, don't you?
PETER	Oh yes, I see. I've worked my guts out for you for two years and now it's half time. Well, I'm sorry, but I'm leaving. I'll get another job, full time.
MR TURNER	Well, if that's how you feel, you can go. Pack up your things and go to find another job, if you're lucky.
TEACHER	So Peter leaves, but then he thinks perhaps he'd be better to go home.
PETER	Jonathan's doing OK, living in a warm home, where I've been out in the cold and wet every day. He's got a cushy job. Yes. I'll go home. I'll text them.
MRS BARNES	(*on the phone to Mr Barnes*) Yes, I've just read Peter's text. He's coming home. Oh, isn't that wonderful? We must celebrate his homecoming. Yes. Tomorrow. I'll get his favourite dinner. I'm so excited.

The next day, the Barnes' home.

MR BARNES	It must almost be time for the train. I'll go down to the station and be there ready for him. I bet he'll have a lot to tell us.
MRS BARNES	I can hardly wait. His favourite meal will be ready for him at one o'clock. Oh, I feel so excited. Jonathan is coming home to lunch too and I'll have you all together again.

MR BARNES	Don't get too excited. You'll embarrass him.
MRS BARNES	I know, but it's difficult to be calm today.
MR BARNES	Yes, well, I'd better be off. I want to get to the station before the train arrives. (*Mr Barnes goes off as Mrs Barnes starts to gather things for laying the table.*)

Some time later, the Barnes family, including Jonathan but not Peter, are seated at the table.

JONATHAN	Well, where is this wonderful brother of mine?
MRS BARNES	He'll be down in a moment. He went to get a shower.
JONATHAN	What a welcome he gets. His favourite roast, kept waiting while he has a shower. Champagne, wine. What has he done to warrant such a fuss? He went away when it suited him, and now comes back when it suits. Probably broke. All this while I've been slaving away in an office. Have I ever had such a fuss made of me? No. Just because he's decided to come home, he's treated like royalty. It isn't fair.
MR BARNES	Hang on, Jonathan. You are no less loved and welcomed in your home, and you know that one day everything I have will be yours, but your brother was lost to us for two whole years and more, but now he is home. That really is a cause for celebration.

That little play represents the Bible story of The Prodigal Son.

209

Questions

1. Do you think Jonathan was justified in his annoyance that his brother had returned and was so welcomed? Write a letter to your friend about it, showing whether or not you agree with him.
2. What sort of a person was Peter? Do you think he deserved to be so welcomed? Discuss your views with a partner.
3. If you had the choice, where would you rather work? Write your answer, giving reasons for your choice.

THE STORIES OF KING ALFRED AND KING CANUTE

PROPS required for the King Alfred scene: a table laid for a meal, a mock fire, some cakes. For the King Canute scene: a chair.

When the children have come into the class the teacher tells them they are going to hear some stories about two Saxon kings.

CHILD   What were their names, Miss?

TEACHER   The first one you will learn about was called Alfred and the second one was called Canute.

CHILD   When did they live, Miss?

TEACHER   A long time ago. King Alfred in the 9th century (AD 840 to 899) and King Canute was later (AD 995 to 1035).

CHILD   What did they do, Miss?

TEACHER   Well, listen and you will find out about them. Those of you who have learned about the Vikings will remember Alfred and the Danelaw, when Alfred made a deal with Gulthorm. Well, after that, even though it seemed that the Vikings had calmed down, they were still ready for battle and although he did not know it, they were keeping track of the King's movements. Listen and you'll know what happened.

CAST

VIKINGS 1–4
KING ALFRED
SERVANT
FEMALE SERVANT
PEASANT WOMAN
COURTIERS 1, 2 & 3
KING CANUTE

VIKING 1   The King has no idea that we know where he is.

VIKING 2   And what he is doing.

VIKING 3	Soon we will creep up on him and capture him.
VIKING 4	What a prize, eh?
VIKING 1	Christmas will soon be here and we know where he will be. Should we get him now?
VIKING 2	No, let us wait until he's lulled by his religion at Christmas. Then we'll strike. (*They all roar with laughter.*) That will give him a shock.
VIKING 3	That's right. And once again we will win the battle.
VIKING 4	That's all very well. We may know where he is, but we must plan how we are going to capture him. He's bound to have some of his Christian soldiers with him.
VIKING 1	Well said, my friend. Come, let us get ready our plan of action. (*They go off in high spirits, feeling pleased with themselves.*)
TEACHER	Meanwhile, King Alfred (known as King Alfred the Great) was quietly enjoying himself with friends at a castle near Chippenham in Wiltshire for Christmas.
ALFRED	A toast. To you all, my friends, and my thanks for the happy time we have spent together. And now, we will take wine to bring in the New Year. May it be more peaceful than the – (*A noise … door banging, running feet.*)
SERVANT	(*running in*) My Lord, horsemen, many of them, coming this way. They are riding hard, Sire, flee. They're nearly upon us.
ALFRED	Which way can I go? I cannot be captured.
FEMALE SERVANT	This way, my lord. Down the steps, to the cellar. There's a passage from the back wall. Quick. It will take you to the back of the

	castle. I've sent to say your horse must be ready for you. Go, sir, and God speed.
ALFRED	My thanks. Farewell.
TEACHER	Safely away, he outwitted the Vikings, though as he went he heard...
VIKING 1	(*banging on the door*) The King. Come out.
TEACHER	He did not stay to hear the rest, but galloped his horse as fast as it would go to the safety of the Somerset Levels. By then it was daylight and he stopped to rest when he saw an old peasant woman tending her fire outside her poor cottage.
KING	Madam, I have ridden a long way and my horse and I are exhausted. May we beg some water?
PEASANT	You look a right ruffian. The water barrel is over there. Help yourself.
KING	Thank you.
PEASANT	Anyway, what's a wretch like you doing with a grand horse like that? Steal it, did you?
KING	No, I assure you. The horse is mine.
PEASANT	Mm. Well, I can't stay talking to you, vagabond or whatever you are. I've got work to do. You say you are exhausted, well you can sit awhile and while you're sitting you can watch my cakes I've just put to cook on the fire. I must go and milk my cow. Watch them, mind. Don't let them burn.
KING	As you say, Madam. I'll look after them for you.

(*Peasant goes off. The king sits by the fire.*)

TEACHER   But he didn't watch the cakes and the peasant woman came back as the cakes were burning.

PEASANT   Why, you good for nothing. You've let my cakes burn. Get out of my sight, you, you... Who are you anyway?

KING   I know you do not recognise me and I deserve your scolding. But, I am so concerned for the safety and well being of my country.

PEASANT   Recognise you? Your country? But, oh God save me. You're the King, you must be ... oh, forgive me, fool that I am. But how did you come to be here?

KING   That is a long story, but in brief I was fleeing from enemies who would capture me.

PEASANT   Then, my Lord, stay here. My husband will insist when he returns.

KING   Thank you, good peasant, but I must leave. I have to find a way to bring God's peace to our country. Farewell and thank you.

CHILD   Did the peasant woman forgive him?

TEACHER   We don't really know. In fact, we don't even know if the story is true but it is one of those strange legends that sometimes appear in history, which seems almost to be true. But it's odd, that even though Alfred was the only English king to be called 'The Great' King of Wessex and England and he did a great deal to bring peace to the country, as well as furthering the Christian religion, he seems to be remembered more for the burnt cakes than for anything else.

CHILD   That was a good story, Miss.

CHILD   Are you going to tell us about the other king?

215

TEACHER   Yes I am. But this is different. Again, we have no idea how true it is, but there is a message within it, which perhaps we should all share. King Canute was loved by his subjects and they thought he was so wonderful he could do anything, even make the sea obey him. So this is what happened.

COURTIER   What a wonderful man our King Canute is. He keeps peace in our land, his rule is fair, he does all he can for the poor.

COURTIER 2   I agree. He is very modest and doesn't realise how clever he is.

COURTIER 3   Why, I believe he could even control the waves of the ocean.

COURTIER 1   That's taking it a bit too far, don't you think?

COURTIER 3   No I don't. You all admire him. I say he could do it.

COURTIER 2   Very well, we will ask him to go down to the beach.

CANUTE   Did I hear 'go down to the beach'?

COURTIER 2   Yes, Sire. We are saying that you could control the waves.

CANUTE   Are you indeed? Very well, we shall go down to the beach. Bring my chair, someone.

COURTIER 3   I will carry it, Sire.

CANUTE   Right. Place it near to the oncoming waves.

TEACHER   And that is what they did. And King Canute cried.

CANUTE   Back you waves. Back, I say. It is my command and I am the King.

TEACHER   But the waves kept coming. So he said again,

216

CANUTE   Back waves. Back, I say. It is my command and I am the King.

TEACHER   But the waves kept coming and they splashed over the King and made him wet all over. Well, as we know that's what waves do. So the King turned on his courtiers and said:

CANUTE   You flatterers. Stupid people. I know what you were doing, trying to flatter me, for your own ends I'll be bound. Get you hence and remember this. No earthly being, king or vagabond can control the waves. There is only ONE who can make both wind and waves obey. So, get you gone all of you.

TEACHER   And all the courtiers went away, feeling very ashamed of themselves and vowing to remember

217

what the King told them. There is only ONE
who can make the wind and waves obey.

So, children, that was the lesson in the story.

CHILD   Was that story true, Miss?

TEACHER   Well, like King Arthur, King Canute did exist,
but we really do not know if this story is true
either. But it is one that has been handed down
to children for many years.

Questions

1. Where was Alfred when the Vikings appeared?
2. How did Alfred escape?
3. Where did he go?
4. When he saw the peasant, what did he ask for?
5. What did she call him?
6. What did she tell him to do?
7. Do you know if this is a true story? How?

Questions

1. Why did King Canute tell the waves to obey him?
2. What happened when he tried?
3. What did he call the courtiers?
4. Who did Canute say could control the wind and the waves?

TOLERANCE – A DISCUSSION GAME

When the children come into the classroom and settle down, the teacher tells them that they are going to play a game which will give them a chance to practise their speaking skills.

She/he then asks the children to take a partner. When this is done the pairs are given pieces of card on which are printed opposing words. For example, on one card could be 'vegetarian' and on the other 'meat eater'.

After allowing the children time to think about it, each pair takes turns to praise the one on his/her card. The object of the game is to try to convince the other of the merits of one against the other, but at the end, accepting that there is good in both, showing tolerance, they shake hands and part.

Obviously, the teacher can provide many opposing pairs but here are a few to start.

TENNIS/FOOTBALL WALKING/CYCLING WATCHING TV/READING HOLIDAYS ABROAD/IN THE UK ART/SPORT SCHOOL/HOME

This kind of work could be presented at the end of the term, when children can be restless in 'proper lessons'. Whether each pair 'practises' first or plunges straight in will obviously be decided by the teacher, as will the time allowed for thinking and presenting.

A CONSCIENCE GAME

This is a card game for children to help them to be aware of the part played in our lives by the voice of our conscience. The children should be in small groups and the suggestions could be written on the board or pre-prepared. Depending on your perception of the level of understanding in your class, each group could be asked to take three or four cards/suggestions.

In the first of the following incidents, individual children could mime the situation in the shop while a small group of three watch and note how the individual deals with the situation.

THE FOLLOWING QUESTIONS ARE INTENDED TO BE ACTED OUT (IMPROVISATION)

The game is intended to give the children practise in thinking, discussing, writing, speaking and miming.

To the pupils

The dictionary definition of the word CONSCIENCE is a moral sense of right and wrong as affecting a person's behaviour.

Now play the game with the cards /suggestions as follows:

1. You have seen something in a shop which you have been longing for for a long time. You haven't enough money, but since no one is looking it would be easy to take. What would you do?

Groups of four. One child is the one who is tempted and three watch to see how he/she reacts. Then at the end of the class, there is a 'recap' of what happened.

2. You happen to be following an elderly lady and you see her drop a £10 note. She isn't aware that she has done so. So you could pick it up and keep it because you want to buy your friend's birthday present. Do you?

Two children, and one playing an elderly lady. Act out the scene in which you decide what you will do.

3. You have seen a friend help herself to a DVD in the music store. Do you: a) tell her to put it back, b) tell the shopkeeper, c) say 'well done' and take one yourself, d) Tell the police, or e) just walk away?

In groups of five, one child is the thief, one the witness, and the other three children discuss the alternatives, for and against.

4. Your mum has told you to come straight home from school as she has to go out and so she has asked your nan to stay with you. She is to get your tea for you and your mum says she always worries if you're not home to eat it when it is cooked. Mum stresses that it is unkind to worry Nan. But on the way home, you're asked to play football with some mates. You are very tempted to stay with them. So what do you do?

Acting the above scene outside school

CAST

MOTHER
BOY/GIRL, told to get home quickly
BOYS/GIRLS, playing football

MOTHER   (*to boy/girl*) Now, I shall be out when you
               come home from school but your nan will be
               there to get your tea. You must go straight
               home because she gets very worried if you
               are late. Understand?
BOY/GIRL   Yes, OK.
MOTHER   Promise?
BOY/GIRL   Yes.
MOTHER   Good.
               (*Later, after school.*)
CHILD PLAYING FOOTBALL   Hallo. Come and play football
               with us.
BOY/GIRL   I can't, sorry.
CHILD   Why not? Come on.
BOY/GIRL   No, I really shouldn't. I promised.
CHILD   Shouldn't? Who says? Who made you promise?
BOY/GIRL   My mum.
CHILD   Where is she?
BOY/GIRL   She's gone out.
CHILD   Well, she won't know, will she?
BOY/GIRL   No, but...

So get together with a few others in your class and between
you decide what to do.

5. You are staying at a friend's house, and unluckily you
   have broken a rather pretty ornament because you picked

it up to look at it and then dropped it. No one saw it happen so you could get away with it. But, do you? Or do you confess?

Individuals miming the dropping of the ornament. How will you react? This time write about the incident, finishing with your solution.

6. You are playing basketball in a friend's garden and suddenly the ball you have just thrown has smashed a window in his parent's house. His dad comes out and blames him, saying he will have to pay for it himself. Do you: a) keep quiet, or b) tell his dad how you did it?

Three actors. You, your friend, his dad. Act out the scene on the card. This time imagine the scene and make up your own words, making it a little scene like the others.

In small groups, think about and try to answer the following questions.

1. Are we born with a conscience?
2. If we are how does it affect us?
3. If not, how do we obtain one?

When you have thought about these three questions (whether or not you have answered them), write a short piece about how you think you might develop your conscience.

224